Wh...   ...ger?

Was ... ... Was she warm and eager or cool and reserved? Marcus had no idea.

He was hoping for the former as he stared at her mouth.

"The thing about a near-death experience," he said, "is it makes you wonder what you're missing out on. It makes you want to live in the moment more, and do whatever the hell you feel like doing." Would that explanation give her enough warning for what he was about to do?

"Oh, yeah? What else do you think you've been missing out on?" Ginger asked.

"You." He hadn't meant to say it, but half a bottle of wine would do that. Still, it was true. Sitting there right now, he couldn't think of anything on earth he was more curious to experience than Ginger.

Dear Reader,

I love stories of second chances. Whether it be a near-death experience, a love lost then found, a phone call that changes one's life forever—or all three, as is the case in *The One That Got Away*. Such events have the power to transform people. I very much enjoyed exploring how Ginger, Marcus and Izzy are changed by each other and the events that bring them together.

Marcus, especially, is a man who needs to grow. Throughout the writing of this story, I imagined how it would feel to wake up in the hospital, having escaped death, and realize that no one cares enough to rush to his bedside. How would this change the choices he makes the second time around?

I love to hear from readers. You can reach me at jamiesobrato@yahoo.com or via my Web site, www.jamiesobrato.com, where you can also learn more about me and my upcoming books.

Happy reading!

Sincerely,

Jamie Sobrato

The One That Got Away
Jamie Sobrato

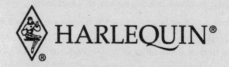

TORONTO • NEW YORK • LONDON
AMSTERDAM • PARIS • SYDNEY • HAMBURG
STOCKHOLM • ATHENS • TOKYO • MILAN • MADRID
PRAGUE • WARSAW • BUDAPEST • AUCKLAND

Recycling programs
for this product may
not exist in your area.

ISBN-13: 978-0-373-71641-8

THE ONE THAT GOT AWAY

Copyright © 2010 by Jamie Sobrato.

This edition published by arrangement with Harlequin Books S.A.

For questions and comments about the quality of this book
please contact us at Customer_eCare@Harlequin.ca.

www.eHarlequin.com

Printed in U.S.A.

ABOUT THE AUTHOR

Jamie Sobrato lives with her two children in a Northern
California town not so different from Promise, where
she is at work on her next book. She loves to hike
and read good books, but not at the same time.
The One That Got Away is her twentieth novel.

Books by Jamie Sobrato

HARLEQUIN SUPERROMANCE
1536—A FOREVER FAMILY
1604—BABY UNDER THE MISTLETOE

HARLEQUIN BLAZE
237—ONCE UPON A SEDUCTION
266—THE SEX QUOTIENT
284—A WHISPER OF WANTING
316—SEX AS A SECOND LANGUAGE
328—CALL ME WICKED
357—SEX BOMB
420—SEDUCING A S.E.A.L.
490—MADE YOU LOOK

To Annabella Sobrato, who reminds me every
day how to live life with joy and passion

PROLOGUE

Berkeley, California
Fourteen Years Ago

ONE MORE DRINK, and she would tell him.

Just one more very stiff drink, and he would finally know how she felt about him.

Terror, like a knife, sliced through her. Which was ridiculous. Marcus Kastanos was Ginger's best friend. She was closer to him than she was to any of her girlfriends. Often she didn't even know what she felt about things until she'd talked them over with Marcus. She shouldn't be hiding her feelings from him now, when it mattered most.

Maybe she should switch from beer to tequila.

She tried to get the bartender's attention by waving her empty beer bottle at him, but it was the end of the school year and the place was busy. He was focused on pouring drinks for a rowdy group celebrating graduation at the other end of the bar.

Her last night on campus, Ginger thought. She felt a torrent of mixed emotions. She was ready to move on after four years at UC Berkeley. She had completed her Bachelor's degree and was excited about starting grad school in Iowa in the fall to earn her Master of Fine Arts; getting into such a prestigious program had been a dream come true. But she also had to confront the fact that she had no home to go back to for the summer.

Her grandmother Townsend, who'd raised her since the death of her parents when she was nine, had died six months ago, and Ginger had no close family left. Marcus was leaving, too, on a trip around the world. This was the first summer she would be truly alone, and that left her feeling empty and scared.

"You look like you need another drink," Marcus said as he sat back down on the bar stool next to her. He'd just returned from the jukebox, where he'd spent the past few minutes pondering music selections.

"I definitely need another," she said, holding up the third bottle of Corona she'd emptied in the past hour. "But I'm making the next one a shot of Don Julio. Care to join me?"

He looked surprised. Marcus knew she didn't do shots unless she was totally stressed.

"Damn straight I'll join you."

Ah, Marcus. She could always count on him to make her feel better. At least for the moment.

She watched as he caught the bartender's attention, and she felt a mixture of affection and annoyance that the man immediately responded to tall, good-looking Marcus while he'd ignored, plain, wallflower Ginger. But that's how it always was—Marcus turned heads, while Ginger faded into the background.

With his adorably shaggy brown hair, piercing green eyes and naturally beautiful body, he was by far the prettier of the two of them. He was the beautiful swan to her ugly duckling. But Marcus saw past her frizzy hair and the extra pounds she tried to hide under baggy sweatshirts. He knew who she was on the inside. In fact, she was convinced he was the only person who truly understood her.

Unfortunately, he was dating someone else.

No sense in dwelling on the negative, though.

Not when this was the night. After four years together, she'd finally found the courage to tell him about the longing—and yeah, lust—she'd been feeling for him for so long she couldn't even remember when it had started. And okay, he might be surprised, but she was sure she hadn't misread the signals he'd been sending her lately.

Hadn't he said just yesterday that she meant the world to him? That she'd made his four years of college the best years of his life? He had never talked that way to her before, and she'd felt something significant shift between them. Surely she hadn't misread his meaning.

No, she was pretty sure he felt more for her than mere friendship.

He glanced over and flashed her a dazzling, heart-melting smile.

Yes. He definitely did. She could see it in his smile. And just as soon as she downed that shot, she'd tell him.

He slid one of the tequilas the bartender poured for him across the counter to her, and she buzzed with warm affectionate feelings.

"To graduation," he said, lifting his own glass to toast.

Ginger raised hers in return, then downed the drink in one long, fiery swallow. Marcus did the same beside her. Thank heaven for the agave plant and whoever had figured out how to make it into a beverage.

The burn of the liquor in her throat turned into

an overwhelming sensation of well-being and invincibility. It was just what she needed.

She could do this. She could tell Marcus how she felt.

She was going to do it.

Right now. This was it.

She caught his eye and let her gaze linger.

"You know," she said, leaning in close, "I've never had the guts to say this before, but I really love you."

There.

She'd done it.

The words had come out so easily, so naturally, she could hardly believe she'd waited this long. And when his eyes warmed in reaction, and his calm, easy manner remained unchanged, she knew she'd done the right thing.

He really did feel the same.

Joy sprang up in her chest like a geyser, and she wanted to leap off her bar stool and throw her arms around him.

He grinned, affecting the wavering posture of a falling-down drunk. "I love you too, *man*." He slurred the words purposefully. "You're the best."

His teasing performance shocked her back into sobriety.

He thought she was joking.

He didn't get her true meaning.

Oh, God. He didn't get it.

Heat rushed to her face.

She was the world's biggest fool. They'd been friends for years, and she'd never once had the guts to tell him the truth. Then yesterday, when he'd spouted a few clichéd words of affection, she'd grasped on to them desperately, convincing herself they'd held a deeper meaning, when all he'd really meant was that he was glad he'd had her as his emotional sounding board throughout college.

She was a fool and an even greater coward, hiding her true feelings behind their friendship. And she was never going to be happy.

Ever.

"Marcus!" a female voice cried from right behind them.

They both turned to find Marcus's girlfriend, Lisette Grayson, standing there, hands on hips, pretty face contorted into a frown.

"Why didn't you meet me at the apartment like I asked?"

"Is it that late?" Marcus glanced at the Budweiser clock on the wall, confused. "I'm sorry. I didn't notice the time."

He stood up from the bar stool and fished his wallet out of his pocket, then tossed a couple of twenties on the bar. "I'm sorry to rush off, Gin."

"It's okay," she lied, trying to put on a carefree expression.

Lisette, who'd never bothered to say more than five words at a time to her, simply turned and marched out of the bar, knowing without a doubt that Marcus would follow.

How did she get such confidence?

Ginger supposed it came with blonde hair, blue eyes, perfect features and a size 4 body.

Marcus paused, flustered. "She's still pissed that I'm going off on a trip."

Ginger knew exactly how Lisette felt. She didn't want to see Marcus go traipsing around the world for a year, either. Knowing him the way she did, she suspected he'd never come back. He'd find a nice little spot far away from the complications of real life and live happy as a clam. She'd been foolishly hoping that confessing her feelings to him would keep him from going—or even more foolish, cause him to invite her along.

But this was Marcus she was talking about. Thanks to his world-traveling hippie parents, he'd learned never to sit still for long. They'd taught him that the best solution to every problem was to leave it behind and ride off into the sunset.

"I guess this is goodbye, huh?" he said.

Tears sprang to Ginger's eyes. She didn't want to cry, not now. She refused to be the kind of girl that clung pathetically to a guy as he walked away. It was time for her to learn from her mistakes. She was never again going to let herself want someone who didn't want her.

"I guess so," she said, then hid her misery behind a fake smile.

"My flight to Paris leaves at six in the morning."

"I could drive you to the airport," Ginger offered, kicking herself even as she said it. She already knew Lisette had claimed the job.

"That's okay. You sleep in. You've earned it."

"Write to me, okay?" She hoped she didn't sound desperate.

He smirked. "I'll try. I'm not such a great correspondent."

"Take care of yourself, and come back, okay?" She said, refusing to accept that this might be the last time she ever saw him.

"You're asking a lot."

She laughed, though it came out sounding

forced. "Okay, don't take care of yourself, and don't come back."

"I think I can manage that."

He leaned in and gave her a long hug. Ginger clung to him as if her life depended on it.

Don't go, she wanted to beg. *Don't leave me here alone.*

"Try not to embarrass all those losers at the Iowa Writer's Workshop, okay?" He gave her shoulders a light squeeze as he released her.

"Oh yeah, like that's going to happen."

His smile disappeared. "You're brilliant," he said, sounding more serious that she'd ever heard him before. "Don't let any of those smug bastards convince you otherwise."

Ginger fought to get words past the lump in her throat. "This isn't goodbye, right? We'll see each other again, so no goodbyes."

He kissed her on the cheek, smiled and walked away.

CHAPTER ONE

MARCUS KASTANOS SAT on the set of the British news talk show *London Daily,* sweating a little under the glare of stage lights as hundreds of eyes from the studio audience stared at him.

He didn't consider promotion fun under the best of circumstances—and these were anything but ideal—but he knew his book was good. The story he'd told was an important one that people needed to hear, and for that reason, he'd do everything he could to make sure it got the exposure it deserved. The critical acclaim he'd received was nice, but it meant little if readers didn't know about the book and buy it.

Of course, the death threats were just about the best book promotion money couldn't buy.

If anyone had told him five years ago that he'd be living with a death sentence hanging over his head, he'd have laughed.

He still had trouble believing it.

But checking the street before he stepped outside, triple locking his doors, keeping his curtains drawn at night and traveling with a bodyguard had all become second nature for him the past year, ever since he'd first received the threats.

This wasn't his first time appearing on TV to talk about the political fallout from his novel, but today he felt more uneasy than he usually did, and he couldn't say why. He'd looked out his hotel room window that morning at the gray London sky and felt a bleak mood settle over him along with a more familiar restlessness. Probably the black mood and the edginess were inherited from his father.

The terrorist attacks in London in the past year only added to the anxiety that niggled constantly at the back of his mind.

But no matter. He was here, and he had his book to promote. *Seven Grains of Sand* had just come out in trade paperback a year after its hardcover release, and he wasn't going to cower in fear. The story had to be told.

"And we're on again in five, four, three, two, one…"

"Today we're here with American expatriate author Marcus Kastanos, talking about his controversial novel *Seven Grains of Sand,* and the death threats issued against him as a result of the book's publication."

The host, a man named Liam Parkinson, paused as the live audience applauded. Then he turned to Marcus.

"Thank you for joining us, Marcus."

"Glad to be here."

"As I read your book, I found myself wondering what led you to write a story about a Muslim woman struggling to shed her family's traditions. I'm guessing the book wasn't inspired by personal experience."

Marcus forced himself to grin at the question he'd already answered a million times. "In a sense, it *was* personal experience that led me to tell this story. I was involved in my twenties with a woman whose life wasn't unlike the heroine's in my novel. Her story always haunted me, and I've never been able to shake the anger I felt on her behalf when I listened to her describe what she'd gone through as a child growing up with the painful effects of female circumcision."

"Ah, yes. One of the more graphic parts of the novel—your description of that brutal procedure. Did you do any firsthand research?"

"Most of my research came from my former lover, who encouraged me to write the book, and medical and journalistic articles. I also had several people more familiar with the process than I am read the book for accuracy."

"And what about the now famous death threats? How has your life changed since you first received them?"

Another predictable question, but one Marcus couldn't really answer without putting himself in further danger.

"I'm a bit limited in where I go and what I do these days. I've also scratched all plans to travel to certain Middle Eastern or African countries."

Uneasy laughter from the audience.

"And how do you feel about—" The host's question was interrupted by the sounds of a scuffle in the audience and raised voices.

Marcus peered in that direction and caught the glint of light off metal. This couldn't be happening. Before he could react, the first shot exploded. Then another, and another.

Searing pain in his chest registered only after he was thrown backward against the chair.

In the uproar that followed, his sense of reality became a series of fractured images.

A hand. A leg.

The overhead lights were too bright.

Hey. He was lying down? Why?

Shouting. People all around him were shouting. He had to get up. See what the noise was about.

Ouch. Moving hurt.

His chest, wet and warm. And so painful.

Had he been shot?

He closed his eyes. Yeah. That was better. The noise and pain faded.

He was a kid. Playing. But where? Right. The commune. Oregon. That was chill, man.

No. Not Oregon. Amsterdam. High school. He was so mad. Just so pissed off at the world and his useless father. Didn't get out of bed for days. Depressed. Whatever.

Bed. Bed… Nice. All those hot girls. Berkeley. Good times. Classes. Lit. All those beautiful words. Pulling him in. Inspiring him…

Pounding out that stupid novel. Hours at the freaking computer. Hated it. Every painful second. But he had to do it…even if it hurt.

No. His *chest* hurt.

And why was it so cold? So freaking cold, and the lights…

The stupid glaring lights…

He closed his eyes.

Just let him sleep.

"MR. KASTANOS? Mr. Kastanos? Can you hear me?"

The woman's voice was unfamiliar. A British accent. A cool hand on his arm.

Marcus opened his eyes to see a nurse staring down at him. "Mr. Kastanos, can you hear me?"

He tried to say yes, but only a faint croak emerged from his throat. He struggled to work his head up and down in some semblance of a nod.

"Good. You're at Queen's Hospital. You've received a gunshot wound, but you're going to be okay."

Received a gunshot wound?

She made it sound as if he'd been given an award for good behavior.

"Marcus, thank God you're okay," said a voice from behind the nurse.

A familiar face hovered over her shoulder.

Who was that guy? He searched for a name to attach to the face.

Graham?

Yeah, that was right. Graham something. The publicist his publisher had hired.

Was he okay? Marcus wondered, struggling to sit up.

It was hardly the word he would have chosen for the way he felt.

"Mr. Kastanos," the nurse said, pressing gently

on his shoulder. "I'll send the doctor in to speak with you in a bit. For now, please keep yourself supine and try to rest."

She exited the room, leaving Graham to stare down at him. After waking up in a hospital bed, Marcus really felt that someone he loved should have been hovering over him with a worried look. Not his publicist, a man with a bulbous nose and the ugliest tie Marcus had ever seen. He'd only met the guy a week ago.

Maybe if he pretended to be asleep again, the publicist would go away. He wanted someone else here.

But who would he even call? Who would come? Annika?

Where was Annika? He tried to remember. As a foreign correspondent, she traveled a lot.

Oh, now he remembered. She was in Beirut.

Not likely she'd drop everything and come rushing to his bedside, especially if he was, as the nurse had said, going to be okay.

"That was a right close one, old boy. But the doctor says the bullet went straight through you, missed all the messy bits and came out the other side."

"The bullet?" he tried to say, but his voice was a croaky whisper.

"What's that?" Graham said, leaning in closer.

"What *bullet?*" This time his voice was slightly more audible.

"You do remember being shot, don't you?"

No. Well, maybe… The flurry of fragmented images in his mind started to make sense.

"Do you remember being on the set of *London Daily?*"

Marcus nodded.

"And do you recall anything that happened—"

"Yeah." He closed his eyes as the memories came hurtling back at him, bringing with them a wave of nausea.

"They caught the bugger, you'll be glad to hear. He's in police custody."

Marcus struggled to formulate the question. "How'd he get a gun…inside…with all the security?"

"Unfortunately, the station's security weren't using metal detectors, so it wouldn't have been difficult to conceal a gun."

"No metal detectors?"

With his public appearance and the death threats issued against him?

"Sorry, old boy. Salman Rushdie was here just last year without incident and has a fatwa on his head. I suppose that made everyone a bit lackadaisical."

Graham pulled up a chair close to the bed and sat

down, then made a loud snorting sound and cleared his throat.

Charming.

"Say, do you want me to call anyone?" he offered. "Family? Friends? Let them know what's happened?"

Marcus closed his eyes. He didn't want to lie here staring at Graham, but he didn't want to be alone right now, either. Yet he had no family, no wife, no girlfriend unless he counted Annika, and he wasn't sure she wanted to be counted. How could he have never realized before that their relationship was pretty much a long-distance sex-buddy arrangement?

He couldn't think of anyone who'd want to jump on a plane and hurry to his side. Sure, he had friends, but...

The reality was, none of his friends were close enough to stay by his bedside.

Not a one.

And he knew why.

He left people behind. It was what he did, what he'd always done. It protected him from ever getting too close to anyone.

And now he had exactly what he'd always thought he wanted—no one. No emotional ties.

He'd succeeded at keeping everyone who ever might have gotten close at an impossible distance.

For the first time in years, he wished he hadn't.

"It'll be on the news," he finally said. "Anyone who cares can see it there."

But who would care, when there wasn't a person in the world who would beckon him to rush to his or her side in a crisis? He supposed he should feel lucky he had his paid publicist to keep him company now. Graham was better than no one.

CHAPTER TWO

"WHAT YOU HAVE HERE is a complete teardown."

Ginger Townsend pinned the contractor with a suspicious gaze, not believing him for a second.

"Excuse me?" she said calmly.

"You got rotting window frames, termite damage, a fifty-year-old roof, water damage, a master bath that needs major work—"

"I'm aware of all that. I told you about those problems over the phone, and I also told you this house has a sound structure that I think is worth preserving."

"Not with them termites." The balding, sun-weathered man tucked the pen he'd been scribbling with in the front pocket of his white T-shirt, and tore an estimate sheet from his note pad.

"There's not a house around here that doesn't have termite damage," Ginger argued. "Mine is limited to parts of the structure that can easily be repaired."

"Far as we *know,* it is. I'm just saying, this ain't gonna be a cheap job by any means. You might be better off starting over at the foundation."

Was the man being honest, or was this just his shtick for seemingly gullible female clients with limited knowledge of home renovations, who'd then rush to pay a fortune for his services?

She looked from him to the house, and they both stood staring up at the slightly sagging roof of the 1920s cottage on Promise Lake that Ginger had bought six months ago. She'd spent her life savings on the little house that was long on charm and short on practical features like central heating and insulation. But there was no way she could finance a full teardown.

"Um, well, thanks for your professional opinion," she said, deadpan.

Thanks a freaking million.

"Just callin' it like I see it."

"What does that mean for my leaky windows?" she dared to ask, already wincing at the anticipated monetary hit.

"Here's my estimate, but like I said…"

Ginger glanced at the figure he pointed to on the sheet and resisted the urge to throttle the man in his Winchell's Contracting shirt. She gritted her teeth and nodded.

It was a moment before she could speak. "Okay then. Guess I'll have to give that some thought," she finally murmured.

"Let me know if you decide to go forward with the repairs. My schedule fills up fast, so I'll need at least a month's notice, maybe more."

When Ginger was alone, she tore her forlorn stare away from the house that had become a money sink, and turned toward the closest neighbor's house. She wanted to talk to Ruby right now to get a bit of perspective. Ruby had known this house for decades, first as the owner and then as a neighbor. She'd know if it really required tearing down or if Mr. Winchell was just trying to drum up big-money work from a new-to-town greenhorn.

Ginger crossed the yard and went through the gate of the white picket fence that surrounded her elderly neighbor's property. Reaching the front steps, she was surprised not to see the older woman already peering out the front door, nosy as ever.

"Ruby?" she called through the open living room window. "Are you there?"

No answer.

"Ruby?" Ginger called again as she knocked on her neighbor's door.

Normally, no more than a single knock was re-

quired. Ruby tended to hover near the window at
the slightest sign of guests, ready to pounce at the
doorknob. With all of her family either dead or
living too far away to drop by for an impromptu
visit, the older woman relied upon neighbors like
Ginger and friends from town for companionship.

Ginger made a point of checking in on Ruby
every other day or so if their paths hadn't crossed
for some reason. Ruby had quickly become like a
grandmother to her during her short time in Promise.

She could hear the TV in the living room blaring,
but detected no other signs of life.

Ginger tried the front door and found it locked. She
knew Ruby tended to leave the rear door standing
open to let in fresh air, so she circled the house, peering
in windows, a sense of dread growing in her belly. No
sign of Ruby, but when she reached the back door, she
could hear water running in the hallway bathroom.
She peered through the screen door and saw that water
was pooling on the hardwood floor of the hallway.

"Hello? Ruby?" she called, more urgently now,
trying the handle of the screen door and finding it,
too, locked.

Her heart pounded as she jerked at the flimsy
plastic handle, willing it to release. Finally, she gave
it a mighty jerk with all her weight, and the latch

snapped open, allowing her inside. She raced through the kitchen to the hallway, stepping carefully over the pooling water and into the bathroom, where she could see Ruby sitting on the floor in a green terry-cloth robe.

She was conscious, leaning against the bathroom wall. Water flowed over the top of the tub and onto the white linoleum floor around her.

"Ruby, are you okay?" Ginger said as she stepped around her and turned off the water.

"Oh? Hmm?" Ruby looked up at her. "What are you doing here, Ginger?"

She knelt down next to the older woman, her throat tight and her heart pounding. "Are you hurt?" she asked. "What happened?"

"Oh dear." Ruby frowned, looking more annoyed than hurt. "What on earth are you doing here?"

"I was about to ask you the same thing. Did you fall?"

"It's just terrible getting old." Her neighbor sounded disgusted.

"Have you hit your head?" Maybe Ruby was disoriented from a fall. That would explain why she was just sitting there while water flooded her hallway.

"No, no. I forgot I was filling the tub for my

bath, and when I came in, my feet went right out from under me."

"Did you hit anything on the way down?"

"Only my tailbone. I've been sitting here trying to decide if I feel like getting up again."

"Let me get some towels and dry the floor first, okay?"

Ginger opened the bathroom cabinet and pulled out an armful of towels, which she scattered on the floor around Ruby. Then she began sopping up the water. Ten towels later, she had the bathroom and hallway floors dry and had created a mound of sopping-wet towels in the now-drained tub.

"Okay, ready to stand up?"

It was disconcerting to see Ruby, normally spry and energetic, sitting on the floor looking so vulnerable. It reminded Ginger far too much of the other losses she'd suffered in her life—her parents, her grandmother. She didn't want to lose Ruby on top of everyone else.

"Don't you dare tell anyone about this," the elderly woman said as she extended her hands for help.

"My lips are sealed." Ginger knelt, placed her arms under Ruby's and carefully lifted her. She was surprised at how light the woman felt.

"I'm soaked," Ruby grumbled, sounding a little more like her old self.

"How does your tailbone feel? Do you think you can stand unsupported?"

"Let's give it a try."

Ginger let go, keeping her hands close in case Ruby became unsteady again. But she was standing firm, trying to straighten her soggy robe.

"Okay, now let's find you some dry clothes."

Her neighbor waved away the offer of help. "I'm fine. You go make us some tea and I'll get dressed."

"I'd better walk you to the bedroom," Ginger insisted, not convinced she could manage on her own. But Ruby was already elbowing past her, unwilling to be treated like an invalid.

Ginger gave a sigh of relief. That was more like the woman she knew and loved. She followed her down the hall to find the bedroom door swinging shut in her face.

"Let me know if you need any help," she called, then went back to the kitchen. The living room television was still on, and could be heard throughout the house, blaring the latest headlines on CNN. Ruby claimed the noise kept her company.

Ginger checked the kettle for water and turned on the burner under it. Then she got out cups, saucers, sugar and milk.

A moment later, Ruby came into the kitchen, already dressed.

"I'm sorry I'm such a mess—haven't had a chance to do my hair yet." She patted at the unyielding white bob that appeared only slightly less kempt than usual.

"You look fine," Ginger assured her. "I want you to let me know if you start to feel bad because of your fall. I'll take you to the E.R. anytime you want, okay?"

Ruby waved a dismissive hand. "Would you stop fussing over me and tell me why you had that work truck in your driveway first thing this morning?"

"I had a contractor over to look at the house and give me an estimate on some repairs. He said I need to tear down the place and start over."

Ruby scoffed. "These contractors—they all want your money. That house is as sturdy as the day it was built."

"That's exactly why I came over—to ask you what you thought." Ruby had lived in the cottage as a child and had been its owner until she sold it to a family twenty years ago. The parents, as they'd aged, hadn't kept up with repairs, and Ginger had bought the house from them knowing it was a fixer-upper—or at least that's what she'd thought.

Now she knew the full extent of what that term meant.

Two months ago a leaky roof and window, a few weeks after that a burst pipe in the kitchen wall. Then the discovery of termites, and the most recent surprise—most of the wood floor in the bathroom and one closet was rotten and about to give way under the weight of the tub and sink.

But oh, how beautiful the house was. Its pale weathered wood siding and gingerbread trim had a charm completely absent from any other home she'd ever had, and she loved the place deep down, as if it were a family member. Which explained why she'd been so put off by the contractor. It was as if he were advising her to pull the plug on Grandma.

Before Ginger could thank Ruby for her reassurance, a familiar name blared into her consciousness from the TV in the living room. She perked up her ears.

...*author of the controversial novel* Seven Grains of Sand, *shot on the set of a London morning news show*...

Marcus? Had they just said Marcus Kastanos? Her Marcus?

Shot?

That's exactly what the report had said.

The news ricocheted around her brain for a startled moment, before her heart began beating double time and the reality of the words sank in.

She swung around and hurried into the living room, where the TV assaulted her with more awful details.

Terrorist...death threats...book tour...condition unknown...

The television screen now displayed a photo of the only man she'd ever loved, while the reporter stated the facts so dispassionately, they couldn't be real. None of this could be true.

Marcus.

Shot by a terrorist.

Condition unknown.

Suspect in custody...

No.

No, no, no, no, no.

As if she were the one who had been shot, a fast-forward movie of her friendship with Marcus played in her mind. Poetry readings, lazy coffee shop Sundays, hiking Mount Diablo, laughing at episodes of *The Simpsons,* daydreaming about being great writers someday...

"Are you okay, dear?" Ruby said from what felt like miles away. "You look like you've seen a ghost."

But she couldn't reply. She'd been propelled backward into her early twenties, when she'd been a naive girl in love with an undeserving guy. Her love for him had been deep, and heady, but completely foolish. She knew that now.

"Ginger, dear? What on earth is wrong?" Ruby sounded seriously concerned.

"I know him," she murmured.

"What's that?"

Ruby didn't have the best of hearing, and Ginger hadn't spoken loudly enough to be heard over the TV. The anchor had now moved on to a report about the latest financial news.

"I know him," she said again.

Ginger's heart continued to pound double time. She had to get away from the noise of the television, so she walked past Ruby, back into the kitchen.

"You know *who?*" her neighbor asked, following her. "That fellow on the news?"

"Marcus Kastanos. We were best friends in college."

"Well, isn't that the living end." Ruby frowned sympathetically. "I do hope he's okay."

Ginger had known about Marcus's controversial first novel—she'd read it, and thought it was brilliant—and also about the threats. She'd been afraid for him, but she'd never imagined...

It didn't seem possible.

Marcus, whom she hadn't seen since college,

was frozen in time for her, still the laid-back man-child she'd known and loved. But they'd lost touch. Marcus had never come back to the United States from his postgrad trip, and Ginger knew little more about his life than what she'd read in the author bio on his book jacket.

She'd last e-mailed him a year ago, a brief congratulations on his new book, to which he'd sent her a friendly but cursory reply. It hurt to be reminded how far apart they'd grown, so she hadn't made any effort to keep up the correspondence. It was easier not to.

Her hands shaking, she pulled a chair out from the table and sagged into it.

"You just take a few deep breaths," Ruby suggested in a voice meant to comfort. "I'll get you some water."

Marcus.

What if he wasn't okay? What if he—

She couldn't finish the thought, and the rush of emotion she felt at the possibility that he might die surprised her a little. She'd experienced enough death in her life to know all too well how it felt to lose someone she loved, but she didn't love Marcus in any active way now. And yet here she was, reeling as if she'd said goodbye to him yesterday.

This was ridiculous. Had she been kidding herself to think she'd moved on? No. Definitely not.

But still, she had to believe he was going to be okay. He was going to live. There wasn't any way life would deliver such a blow.

Except...she'd received the worst of blows already—the deaths of her parents and grandmother. Ginger knew firsthand how disinterested Fate was in the impact its twists and turns had made on her individual life. If Fate had ever cared for her personally she'd still have the family members she loved. And the words *shooter* and *Marcus* would never have been uttered in the same sentence.

Numbly, she took the glass of water Ruby handed her. Drinking down the cool liquid, she recalled the last time she'd seen Marcus, on the night of their graduation from UC Berkeley.

She'd insisted that night couldn't be a final goodbye, that they would see each other again.

The teakettle began to whistle, and the older woman turned off the stove and started making tea.

God, she'd been so foolish, thinking Marcus had wanted anything but her friendship, Ginger recalled. It still embarrassed her to remember how badly she'd misread him.

"I know!" Ruby exclaimed out of the blue. "He's that fellow, isn't he? The one you said you were in love with?"

There was nothing wrong with Ruby's memory.

"Yes," Ginger said, cringing inwardly.

"The one you said you left your fiancé for, because he could never measure up?"

God, her actions sounded so pathetic when put like that. She'd left Leo for a ghost, for a fantasy, for a love that had never been real, because it had never been reciprocated. But she'd known it was the right thing to do, because she hadn't loved Leo the way she should have—the way she wanted to love a man. And even though she knew Marcus wasn't the right guy for her, she had to believe there really was someone out there with whom she could share equally passionate feelings, not the lopsided kind she'd experienced thus far.

"I'm sorry, Ruby, I'm going to have to take a rain check on the tea." Ginger stood up, still shaky, and placed her now-empty glass by the sink.

"You're not going to go so soon?"

"I need to make some phone calls and find out about my friend," she said, her voice nearly breaking.

"Why don't you wait until you've calmed down a bit?"

"I…I can't. I'll come back in a little while, okay? I'll get all those wet towels out of the tub and hang them outside for you."

"Now don't you worry about that."

"It's okay, I'll come do it. Just give me an hour." And with that she headed out the back door.

She hurried across Ruby's lawn and her own, trying to think what to do. What made the most sense? Who could she call? How could she get in touch with the hospital in London?

How many other people would be thinking the same thing she was?

It wasn't as if Marcus belonged to her.

He didn't. And her feelings were a lost cause, but...

Ginger had long ago accepted her calling as a warrior for lost causes. Her house was a prime example. Any sensible person would have taken one look at the sagging roofline and moved on to buy a nice new house in the suburbs. But Ginger, either too brave or too foolish for her own good, had seen the house's history, its quirky handmade shingles and its beamed ceilings, and she'd been unable to resist the project of reviving it to its former glory.

She had no common sense, her granny Townsend had always said. But Ginger's grandmother, a bit of a romantic like her, had told her she had something better—*uncommon* sense. She'd said she could see things other people couldn't, which made her daring enough to try things other people wouldn't try.

Ginger supposed that was how she'd managed to make her living as a writer and adjunct college instructor. But it was also how she'd ended up with a house that needed more repairs than she could afford.

In all these years, she'd never let herself hope that Marcus might love her back, and she'd forced her heart to let go of the idea. Yet man after man hadn't been able to measure up to him, and now, years later, here she was alone and reeling at the news that he'd been injured.

She wanted to talk to Marcus, to see him, to get some assurance that he was okay. And maybe then she could make sense of this tumult of emotions she was experiencing.

But was she kidding herself? Were her motives really so pure, or did she actually want to see if there was any hope of her love being requited?

She went inside the house and down the hallway, straight to her office. Sitting at her desk, she brought her computer out of sleep mode.

Dear Marcus…

She began composing an e-mail to him in her head. I could hardly believe the news….

She made a face. No. She should call instead.

This kind of event required a phone call. Even an in-person visit. Maybe she'd fly to London. No, no, she was getting way ahead of herself. That was a crazy idea.

She didn't even have his phone number anymore. But she had his e-mail address.

So it would have to be an e-mail, for now.

Dear Marcus, she began again. I was so worried when I saw the news....

CHAPTER THREE

MARCUS LOOKED OUT THE small window as his plane dropped from its cruising altitude and a brown landscape came into view down below. Dry hills, a scattering of tiny houses, the piercing blue California sky all around him for the first time in years.

He should be happy to be returning to the United States. He was alive after the worst ordeal of his life.

One bullet cleanly through. Thirty-two stitches. Two weeks in recovery.

More concerned phone calls than Marcus would have expected, and an in-box full of mostly unread e-mail messages bearing headers such as I'm so glad you're okay! and I heard the news....

He hadn't had the stomach to read his e-mail for a week after getting back home to Amsterdam, because one phone call in particular had left him reeling, and he'd known an e-mail with an attached photo would be waiting for him in his in-box.

And when he'd finally opened it and seen the picture, he'd known it was all true. The face, the spitting image of his own mother as a little girl, was painfully beautiful to him.

It had been surreal hearing Lisette's voice after all these years. But it hadn't been her voice at all. Only one that sounded like hers.

Like hers, but different.

Younger.

The girl had seen the news about him and felt she had to call. She wanted to meet him.

Her name was Isabel.

Isabel Dawn Grayson.

Izzy for short.

She was thirteen years old.

The facts all lined up in his head, neat and orderly, but that didn't mean they made sense. His brain hadn't assimilated the idea that he was a father, that there was a kid in the world with his blood coursing through her veins.

But that hadn't been the only shocking news. Her mother, Lisette, was dead. Died three months ago of ovarian cancer.

Marcus hadn't talked to Lisette in the fourteen years since their breakup after college. Hadn't known he'd left her pregnant with a child. Hadn't even been able to make sense of the hows and whys of it all until a woman named Nina, Izzy's legal guardian and godmother, had gotten on the phone after Izzy and cleared up some of the details.

So now he not only had a daughter he'd never met before, but was also a single father. All in one fell swoop.

The impact of the revelations had left him reeling ever since the phone call, and he'd already been in a state of shock at finding himself flat on his back in the hospital thanks to a lone nut job with a gun.

If Marcus had been the mystical, spiritual thinker his parents had raised him to be, he'd have believed the universe was trying to tell him something big. But one element of his parents' philosophy had gotten through to him: he did believe in Fate. And Fate had handed him not only a second chance at life, but a chance to know the daughter he might never have otherwise met. Fate had made him a father, and he was going to make the best of these new circumstances in his life, no matter how radical a change from his previous reality it all was.

Izzy had said she wanted to spend the summer with him.

Maybe longer.

And he was on his way to meet her and start being her dad.

She'd been living in San Francisco with Nina for the past few months, but she hated the city. She'd spent most of her life on the rural California coast near Santa Cruz with her mom, and she was intimidated by the noise and the hustle and bustle of people everywhere.

The plane touched down on the tarmac of San Francisco International Airport right on schedule, and Marcus's stomach pitched. He was terrified.

No, he couldn't focus on his fear. It was only going to freak him out. He needed to concentrate on the pleasant, comforting parts of returning to the country he'd left.

There was Ginger, whom he'd always regretted losing touch with. She reminded him of his days at Berkeley. Those four years were probably the happiest in his life, and if he hadn't been such a lousy correspondent, he might still have been able to call her his best friend. She'd been the most sincere, solid person he'd ever let himself get close to. She was far more solid than him. He had always felt a little like a dry leaf to her oak tree…as if he might drift away with a strong wind, whereas she was rooted and strong, and would still be standing tall a hundred years from now. He realized that he'd always taken her for granted. She wasn't an oak tree—she was a special person who deserved better than a friend who never called or wrote.

It would be great to see her and catch up on all that had happened in the last fourteen years. And they were going to have a whole summer to do it, since she was opening her home to him and Izzy. He'd felt a little uncomfortable asking if she'd mind letting them stay for a week or so while he looked for a place, but when she'd suggested they stay the whole summer, he was reminded yet again of what a good friend she was. He had ulterior motives: Ginger was the one person he knew who might be able to help Izzy make sense of her mother's death, since she knew what it was like to lose a parent.

Warmth filled his chest when he thought of Ginger's kindness, of how insistent she'd been that having two houseguests for the summer would be no trouble at all.

There. That's what he needed to focus on. Happy thoughts.

Hers had been the most welcome of all the e-mails he'd found waiting for him upon his return to Amsterdam after the hospital stay. He'd called her right away and, without thinking twice, asked her for that huge favor, never really doubting that she'd be willing to help. Now that he'd stared death in the face, he understood the priceless value of such a good friend, and he promised himself he would never take her for granted again.

So she was meeting him at the airport, driving him to pick up Izzy and taking them to her house for the summer.

Ten minutes later he was hauling his carry-on bag through the concourse, following the signs pointing to the baggage claim area.

Taking in the sights and sounds of America again for the first time in so many years overwhelmed Marcus with a rare bout of nostalgia. The orderly bustle of American travelers, the sounds of English being spoken... He'd been in San Francisco International Airport countless times, but this time felt different. It was as if he were running away from his old life and the dangers it held. No, not really running away so much as leaving behind an old life for a new one that Fate had insisted upon.

And perhaps more importantly, there was the feeling of anticipation of what was to come. His life as he knew it was about to be dramatically altered, not by a gunshot wound but a thirteen-year-old girl.

His stomach roiled at the thought. For the first

time, the decisions he made about his life, his career, would affect someone else as much as they affected him. His daughter's life was in his hands, and it was a responsibility he wasn't sure he knew how to handle.

Marcus tried to find solace in the wide-open faces of the Americans he passed. Faces of every color, they held a quality not found in the more cautious, businesslike expressions of the Dutch or other Europeans.

He passed a couple of airport shops and was bombarded by the shiny commercialism that also managed to top that of the Dutch by miles somehow. The products were more numerous, the food more varied, the magazines glossier, the women on the covers more unreal.

And then he was descending an escalator, and his nervous energy doubled. Ginger had said she'd meet him near the escalator outside the baggage area. He scanned the crowd, looking for her signature curly auburn hair. When his gaze landed on a woman with exactly that hair color, for a moment he glanced away, sure it wasn't his old college pal.

But the recognition he'd seen in her own gaze caused him to glance back. Impossibly, it was her.

She looked nothing like she had in college. This woman, this grown-up Ginger….

No, it couldn't be.

But she smiled and waved and called his name. "Marcus!"

It *was* her.

He flashed a confused smile and stepped off the escalator to find himself enfolded in the embrace of a woman he barely recognized. Hugging her back, he fought to overcome his shock at the change in her appearance.

All of a sudden she pulled away. "Oh! I forgot your wound. Is it okay to hug?"

He laughed. "Don't worry. My shoulder is mostly healed. There's still a bit of pain but nothing to mention most of the time."

"Wow," she said, taking a full step back to scan him up and down. "It's so good to see you! You look exactly the same."

"Liar. But look at *you*. I didn't even recognize you."

Ginger blushed. "Oh, well, I guess I finally lost the oversize sweatshirts and perpetual ponytail."

"And the glasses, and—" He stopped short, not sure what else to say except that she simply seemed…different.

She'd always been on the curvy side, and he suspected her generous breasts used to cause her a great deal of embarrassment—hence the bulky sweatshirts that hid her figure. But now she stood proud and tall, her chest lushly displayed in a stretchy green top and her rounded hips accented nicely by a fitted denim skirt.

Her hair, which she wore down, cascaded over her shoulders in luxurious waves, and something about her expression and her posture made it clear that she'd grown up a lot in the years since they'd last seen each other. Gone was the awkward coltishness of her early twenties. She now had the air of a woman who knew who she was and what she wanted.

She shrugged, growing a little self-conscious under his scrutiny. "It's been too long." She turned her attention to the baggage claim area, glancing at the nearest display screen of arriving flights. "Do you have any luggage checked?"

"Nope. I've got everything right here," he said, indicating his laptop bag and carry-on suitcase.

"Still traveling light," she said, laughing.

"Backpacking taught me that."

"And what time do you need to pick up your—" She faltered, probably as shocked as he was at the situation. "Your daughter? What's her name again?"

"Isabel. I told her I'd be there around noon."

"In the Marina District?"

"That's right. The house is off Divisidero. I've got the address in my pocket."

She glanced at the small silver watch on her wrist. "It's almost eleven. Plenty of time."

As they headed for the nearest exit, Marcus resisted the urge to pepper Ginger with questions about her life. He felt bad for not having stayed in touch with her over the years, but he also knew Ginger well enough to realize she probably didn't hold it against him. She knew he was laid-back—maybe even lazy, he admitted—when it came to relationships, but in college she'd easily accepted his shortcomings.

When they reached her car, a white Toyota Prius, she opened the trunk for him to stow his bags.

Once they were in motion, she posed the obvious question as she navigated through the parking garage. "So, how are you feeling about meeting Isabel?"

Marcus's mouth went dry. "I'm terrified, of course. What if she doesn't like me or…"

"Or you don't like her." Ginger filled in the blank.

That was what he'd always loved about her. She could see straight to his heart.

"I wasn't going to say that, but yeah."

She shot him a sympathetic glance. "It's a valid worry, I think."

"You don't have any kids yet, right?"

Ginger barked out a surprised laugh. "No, none for me. I'm pretty sure I'd have already mentioned them if I had any."

"I guess so," Marcus said, wondering if he should pursue the subject. But he'd never felt the need to hold back with Ginger. "I'm surprised. I always thought you'd make a good mom."

"I'm only thirty-five—I've got a few eggs left in me," she joked.

"So you haven't even gotten married, huh?"

"I came close a few years ago, but…" Her voice trailed off uncertainly.

"Who left? You or him?"

"It's hard to say." She frowned, her eyes focused on the road ahead.

"Why'd you break up, then?"

"We were trying to adopt a baby from China, and when we found out we'd have a better chance if we got married, I got cold feet. Then Leo got mad and decided he didn't want to be with me if I didn't want to marry him."

"Wow," Marcus said, his thoughts tripping over what different paths their lives had taken. "I'm sorry."

"It's okay. Better off finding out sooner than later that we weren't right for each other."

"And the adoption? Are you still trying to do that?"

Ginger shrugged. "I'd still like to, but I'm flat broke since buying my house, and foreign adoption is an expensive process."

Silence filled the car for a few awkward moments.

He would have to get to know Ginger all over again, he realized now. She wasn't the same idealistic girl he'd gone to college with. She had a lifetime of experiences that he didn't know about.

"Have you seen any photos of Izzy?" she asked out of the blue.

"Yeah, she e-mailed me one. She's pretty. Dark hair, dark eyes, pale skin. She looks exactly like my mom did at that age."

"Does she look like you at all?"

"She does. It freaks me out a little, I'll admit."

"You have every right to feel scared and freaked out and anything else right now. It's a big deal discovering you have a kid you never knew about, and it's an awful thing that Lisette never told you."

"I guess. I mean, at the time, I'm not sure if…"

He trailed off, ashamed to say the words aloud. He didn't even know if what he was about to say was true, anyway. What *would* he have done if Lisette had told him she was pregnant? Would he have had the courage to stick around and be a father when what he'd really wanted to do was travel the world and be responsible only for himself?

It was an impossible question to answer now.

"I'd like to think that if I'd known about her, I'd have been a good father, but I don't know."

"I'm sure you would have been, Marcus—I don't have any doubt," she said with far more certainty than he felt.

"But Lisette and I were finished anyway. There's no way we could have stayed together for the sake of a baby, and I'm sure that's why she didn't tell me, you know?"

"I know, but it was still despicable not to say anything—not to give you the option of being a part of your daughter's life."

"I guess she was scared. And angry. I got the *Reader's Digest* version of events from a friend of hers who's Izzy's guardian now."

"Sure she was scared, but still…" Ginger's voice sounded a little odd.

If Marcus hadn't known better, he'd have suspected she was uncomfortable with the subject.

As she navigated through traffic, he studied her profile, still stunned at what a beautiful woman she'd become. And yet it was hard to put his finger on anything profoundly different. There were sim-

ply a lot of subtle changes that added up to a pro-
found transformation.

Forcing his gaze away from her so that he
wouldn't be caught staring, Marcus took in the
sights of South San Francisco. This area north of the
airport had never been known for great character or
charm, but he felt a little tight in the chest to be here
again. His parents were bohemian drifters, so he'd
grown up never spending too long in one place, but
cliché as it sounded, his heart had always called San
Francisco home.

And here he was again.

Once Ginger was cruising on the highway and
could divide her attention between driving and
talking again, she cast a glance at Marcus.

"So Lisette died of ovarian cancer?"

"Yeah." A new weight settled on Marcus's chest.

He no longer held any romantic feelings for the
woman, but it hurt in an oddly distant way to know
she was gone. What was more painful, though, was
knowing he'd never be able to talk to her about
Isabel. He couldn't ask Lisette about their daughter's childhood—what her first words were, or what
she'd been like as a little girl, or whether she'd
suffered not having a father around.

That was all lost to him, but he wouldn't lose any

more time with his daughter. Somehow, he had to find a way to fit this child into his life.

"I'm sorry," Ginger said quietly.

"It's weird, you know. If I hadn't been shot in London, I wouldn't have found out that Isabel exists. She wouldn't have contacted me if she hadn't seen the news."

"I'm sure she would have. Maybe not now, but eventually."

"Who knows how many more years I'd have missed out on."

"So it's kind of a weird blessing, what happened, huh?"

"Yeah, I mean, I never would have thought being shot could be a good thing, but in some crazy ways it changed my life."

There was a moment's pause, then Ginger said, "I guess I wouldn't have gotten back in touch with you, either."

"I'm glad you did." That was one thing Marcus had no doubts about. "It was scary, lying in that hospital in London and realizing I didn't have any next of kin to call."

She said nothing, and an awkward silence grew between them. Ginger was too kind to point out the obvious—that it was Marcus's own fault he was close to no one. He might not have had control over the fact that his blood family had dwindled over the years, but he had only himself to blame for not staying in touch with all of his friends.

"Who *did* you call?" she finally asked.

"My publisher—since the book tour had to be cancelled."

"Oh."

Another awkward silence.

"I'm sorry," Marcus finally said, surprised at the emotion in his voice. "It was my fault we lost track of each other, and I really appreciate your helping me out now, even though I don't deserve it."

"It wasn't your fault!" She glanced over at him again, this time incredulous. "I mean, there are two of us here and we're both capable of making a phone call or writing a note."

"Sure, but—"

"There's no point in assigning blame. I'm so glad you're safe and back in the U.S., I don't care what happened, you know?"

Her voice sounded so much like the old Ginger he'd known back in school that he laughed. "I do. There's nothing like a near-death experience to remind you what's important."

"And Isabel," she said carefully. "Do you think she's angry with you?"

"For what?"

"For not being around."

"But how could I have been?"

"That's how an adult would think about things, but a child might see things differently. She might feel betrayed anyway."

Marcus hadn't considered this, and it gave his stomach something new to cramp up over. "I don't know what Lisette told her about me. I guess some of it might not be so great."

"Perhaps. Or even if she didn't say anything negative, Isabel might have read between the lines in an unfavorable way. Who knows?"

"Yeah," he said weakly.

"I don't mean to be pessimistic," Ginger added. "I only want you to be prepared for possible difficulties. Probably things will be fine."

She guided the conversation toward more neutral topics, filling him in on the classes she taught at the community college, the writing she'd been doing, the whereabouts of their college classmates, sprinkling in interesting gossip whenever she had any to share. But Marcus was barely paying attention. He knew she was trying to distract him, to get his mind off more troubling matters, and he appreciated her effort, yet he couldn't keep his thoughts from dwelling on the daughter he was about to meet.

As the minutes ticked by and they made their way through the city toward Isabel, Marcus found himself paralyzed with anticipation and dread the likes of which he'd never experienced before.

Not even the price on his head had scared him like this, because of course, the death threat affected only him. But this—this fatherhood thing—meant that his actions from this point on really mattered, that whatever he did affected not only him, but a child who needed him. A child who'd just lost her mother.

The ride passed too quickly, and when Ginger pulled into the driveway of the address Isabel had given him, he shuddered. A three-story Edwardian row house loomed before them, inside of which his child was waiting.

Okay, deep breaths. In, out, in, out.

He could do this. He could meet her. He wouldn't run away this time.

It was too late now, anyway.

CHAPTER FOUR

IZZY WATCHED THE CAR pull into the driveway, and her stomach did that thing where it felt like it was turning inside out. Then she watched *him* get out of the car. He looked nothing like she'd imagined.

Which was weird, since she'd seen some pictures of him on the Internet. His author publicity photo showed only his face, though, and now, seeing him strolling up Nina's driveway, she realized he was much bigger than she'd thought.

Her mom's last few boyfriends had been small men who talked about wine too much and worried a lot about keeping their shoes neat and their clothes lint free. She'd started thinking that kind of guy was her mom's type or something. She'd started thinking her mom had bad taste in boyfriends.

But this guy...this guy who was supposed to be her dad, Marcus Kastanos—would she want to change her name from Grayson to Kastanos, even though it sounded weird?—he looked like the opposite of a guy who talked about wine and worried about his clothes.

She heard the knock at the door and felt like puking.

Oh, God.

This was it.

Ever since the first moment she'd realized other kids had one dad and one mom or two dads or two moms or a houseful of moms and aunts and whoever else to care for them, she'd desperately wanted to meet her own father.

Well, she'd wanted to and she hadn't wanted to. Her mom had told her stuff. She'd said he wouldn't be a good dad. That he wasn't that kind of guy.

And now he was here, coming to take her off for their own little summer getting-to-know-you party. Why had she even suggested it?

But if he wasn't a dad kind of guy, then what? Should she even go?

She couldn't do it. She didn't know this guy. He didn't know her.

This whole meeting thing was a terrible idea. Why had she phoned him?

She stood up, walked across the room and locked her door.

Then she went into her bathroom and cried.

She buried her face in Nina's thick gray towels to drown out the noise of her pathetic sobbing, she had a moment of totally hating that she was messing up her carefully applied eye makeup, but she kept right on crying.

She hated the guy downstairs for not having stuck around when she was born to get to know her, to find out what a great person she was. He'd just disappeared. He'd been sure he wouldn't love her and he'd taken off.

He was a loser.

Well, maybe that wasn't fair. He hadn't known about her, so she couldn't really blame him for not sticking around.

And she hated her mom for dying. This was the thing she'd never said aloud in her own head before. It was an ugly dark cloud that had been lurking in the back of her brain, waiting for the right moment to move in and make everything even more screwed up.

Izzy sank onto the floor, taking the towel with her. Her chest was doing this weird heaving, shuddering thing, and she needed to blow her nose, and she was drooling.

Not pretty.

She heard someone knocking on the bedroom door and calling for her to come out. It was Nina.

"Izzy? Are you in there? Can you open up, please?"

She didn't have anything against her. Nina was her godmother and her mom's friend, and she'd been nice to Izzy. Too nice, even. Since she didn't have any kids of her own, Nina didn't know what to do with a teenager who'd just landed in her house, motherless and devastated. So she had bought Izzy stuff and tried to soothe her by taking her out to fancy restaurants. She'd even suggested the two of them take a trip to Hawaii or Paris or wherever Izzy wanted to go.

But it was weird. Izzy didn't want anything, and she didn't want to go anywhere. She barely wanted to get out of bed in the morning, but she didn't think about her mother much, either. Whenever a memory of her mom slipped into Izzy's head uninvited, she'd force herself to think about something happy, like her dog, Lulu, when she was a puppy and so small she could fit in Izzy's palm.

Right now Lulu was downstairs in a pet carrier next to her suitcase, waiting to be taken on the trip. Izzy wished she hadn't corralled her in that stupid carrier already. She'd have felt a little better if Lulu was in her lap now, staring up at her with her brown cow eyes.

Why had she freaked out like this? Especially now, after all the other stuff that had happened.

Izzy figured that once a kid's worst fear comes true and her only parent dies, and she survives the pain of it, or at least is pretty sure she's surviving, she starts to think nothing can shake her. She starts thinking maybe she's invincible, like some starry-eyed superhero.

But maybe the opposite happens. Maybe when the worst of it is already over, that's when a person falls apart.

Izzy swiped at the drool on her chin with the towel. Her breathing was coming out all shuddery, and she was pretty sure her face looked so puffy it would take her an hour to get it back to semi-normal.

"Izzy...honey...please open up!"

The "honey" part of Nina's plea sounded a little awkward, because she wasn't the kind of person who called people things like that. Izzy figured that even shortening her name to Izzy, as she preferred, must test Nina's preference for formality. Nina had been good to her, but Izzy could tell her godmother was more comfortable bestowing love on the two cats who loathed Lulu's presence than on a teenager, and Izzy didn't really blame her, since Nina had no kids of her own to practice on.

"Izzy, please let me know you're okay, at least. I'm going to have to pick the lock if you don't."

Oh, God. She wasn't ready to face anyone.

"I'm fine!" she lied, but the weepy sound in her voice told the truth.

She could hear Nina talking to someone in the hallway, and then footsteps retreated down the wood staircase. Izzy knew she couldn't stay hiding out in the bathroom forever, so she pulled herself up and took a good hard look in the mirror.

Yikes.

She splashed cold water on her face, hoping to rid her eyes of some of their puffiness. Then she went to work on repairing her makeup. She didn't wear much—just a bit of mascara, eye liner and blush. Nina insisted she didn't need it, but Izzy thought it made a difference. She figured if she had to go to her own mom's funeral, she got to decide whether or not she wore makeup, and Nina seemed to sort of agree, even though she didn't like it.

There was still a shaky feeling in Izzy's belly when she was done, but she didn't feel quite as bad as before. She guessed she needed to let out some of the sheer terror.

But now…

Now she had to face *him*.

MARCUS HEARD THE SOUND of whimpering and looked down to see that there was something brown and wiggly in the pink duffel bag on the ground. Upon closer inspection, mesh panels revealed what looked like a small dog. He knelt down and murmured some soothing sounds to the dog. He suddenly recalled Izzy asking if she could bring her pet along, though in all the upheaval of the past few weeks as he'd prepared to leave Amsterdam, he'd managed to forget they would have a dog along on the trip.

Had he even asked Ginger if she'd mind having a dog at her house?

"That must be Lulu," Ginger said, her memory obviously better than his. "Do you think she'll bite if we try to get her out?"

"Maybe that's why Izzy has her in this travel bag."

Ginger knelt beside the bag. "She looks harmless enough."

"Famous last words," Marcus joked, in spite of his grim mood.

He could tell by Nina's tone as she called through the door that things weren't going well upstairs. And he had no idea what to do. He didn't know how to be a dad, and he wasn't technically anyone's dad except when it came to biology, so he was pretty sure going up there would only make things worse.

He'd opted to stay put for the moment.

When Nina came back downstairs a few minutes later, her expression twisted in a tense smile, Ginger rose from her perch beside the dog.

"Is she okay?" Marcus asked.

Nina sighed heavily. "I'm sure she's about as okay as she can be given the circumstances. I think she's just having a little bout of cold feet."

"Should I go try to talk to her?" he suggested. "Or maybe leave and come back when she's feeling better?"

"I don't have a clue."

The sound of a door opening echoed down the stairway, and a moment later a pair of feet clad in brown suede moccasin boots came into view. A tall, thin girl with a heavy curtain of dark brown hair descended the stairs. She resembled the photo in Marcus's e-mail in-box, but she didn't.

What took his breath away most was how much she looked like him. Like a small, wiry girl version of him in a purple tunic sweater and skinny jeans.

Big, sad brown eyes so like his own stared back at him, seeming to take in the same truth he'd just registered—that there was no doubt who was related to whom.

"Isabel—I mean Izzy," he said. "Hello."

His voice came out sounding stilted, too formal. Marcus wanted to kick himself. He'd rehearsed this meeting in his head at least ten different ways. He could hug her, or shake her hand, or hold back and see what she was inclined to do, or make a joke to ease the tension, or any number of other things, but not one of them struck him as the right thing to do at the moment.

Izzy solved the problem for him by eschewing contact entirely and kneeling beside the doggy travel bag. She unzipped it and withdrew the tiny brown mutt, which looked to be part Chihuahua and part something else. The dog shivered in her arms as it gazed up at her adoringly and licked at her chin.

"This is Lulu," she said.

Marcus reached out and stroked the dog behind its small, floppy ears, grateful for something to do with his hands. He watched the girl's expression relax as she focused on the dog. Then she glanced nervously at Ginger, the one person in the room she didn't know.

"This is my friend Ginger," Marcus said. "We'll be staying at her house."

Ginger smiled warmly. "It's nice to meet you, Izzy. I think Lulu is going to love playing at the lake. Does she like water?"

Izzy grimaced. "She's afraid of water."

"Oh, well, that's okay," Ginger said.

Nina jumped in to rescue the situation. "Maybe I could help you load bags in the car, Ginger."

The two women each picked up a suitcase and went out the front door, leaving Marcus alone with Izzy.

"I know this is hard for you," he said. "Do you feel okay coming with me now, or—"

"It's fine," she said tightly. "Nina has to leave on her work trip to New York, and she said I can't stay here alone. She wanted me to go with her, but I don't want to."

"I'm glad you found me, Izzy," he said, trying to make eye contact. "We're going to have a good summer getting to know each other."

She avoided his gaze by keeping her focus on the dog, but after a few moments of awkward silence she glanced up at him, and he could see the sheer terror in her eyes. Also a bit of defiance, and a healthy dose of sorrow.

How did he go about making the acquaintance of a hostile teenage girl who'd just lost her mother?

He hadn't a clue.

Perhaps he should have read a book, or consulted an expert, but now it was too late....

"Do you like animals?" she asked.

"Um, yeah, sure."

"Are you just saying that? Do you have any pets of your own?"

"I don't have a pet, no."

"Why not?"

"I guess, you know, it's a big commitment. I travel a lot. It would be hard."

"Kind of like having a kid would be hard?"

"Sure, but—look, I'll have to change my life around a bit, but of course I'm glad to. I want you to feel welcome."

"Nina doesn't like having a dog in the house. She's too nice to say so, but she doesn't."

"Izzy, I'm happy to have your dog live with us, okay?"

"You have to say that."

"I mean it."

He felt off-kilter due to the strong undercurrent in their conversation, not quite sure if they were really talking about whether the girl or the dog or both were welcome in his life.

She glared at him with poorly concealed mistrust, then returned her attention to stroking the dog. Lulu had stopped shivering and was resting comfortably in her arms. Marcus was overcome with a wave of inexplicable gratitude for the mutt's presence.

Ginger and Nina reentered the foyer, and Izzy seemed eager to get going.

"Um, well, we should leave, right?" she asked.

"I thought you'd stay and have coffee," Nina said, glancing nervously around the group.

"Can we just get this over with?" Izzy said. "Your plane leaves in a few hours and I'm going to puke if we have to stand around like this much longer."

Marcus silently agreed with her, but at the same time he didn't want to rush her out the door. It seemed such an abrupt transition from a familiar place and person, to a world of strangers.

Nina sighed. "I guess we'll all avoid the rush-hour traffic if we head out earlier rather than later. Are you sure?"

Izzy shrugged. "Whatever."

She and Nina hugged briefly.

"Call my cell phone anytime you want, okay? Anytime. I mean it."

"Okay," Izzy said, sounding listless.

"I want to hear all about Promise Lake. And if for any reason you need to see me, I'll fly you to New York, or I'll come up to Promise once I'm back, okay?"

"Okay."

They said their goodbyes and piled into Ginger's car, Izzy in the backseat with the dog.

This wasn't going the way Marcus had envisioned. He'd expected a bit more enthusiasm on Isabel's part, maybe a bit more warmth. He hadn't expected sullenness or hostility, which proved how far in over his head he was right now. He didn't know a damn thing about teenage girls, so why did he think he could be a father to one?

He didn't. He hadn't chosen this situation. Not exactly, anyway.

Ginger started the car as the dog whimpered in the backseat.

"Is it okay if Lulu rides in my lap?"

"So long as she doesn't pee all over my seat," Ginger said, smiling into the rearview mirror.

Her light tone was met with steely silence, then the sound of the pet travel bag being unzipped.

"Have you had lunch yet?" Marcus thought to ask.

"No. I'm not hungry."

"I'm famished," Ginger said. "Maybe we should stop on our way out of town?"

"Know anyplace good?" he asked.

"There's a great Puerto Rican place in San Rafael once we cross the bridge. Sound good?"

"Do they allow dogs?" Marcus asked.

"Hmm, I guess not. Oh, but I know a pizza place with outdoor seating. How's that?"

"Perfect." He turned around in his seat. "Sound good to you, Izzy?"

"I said I'm not—"

"I know, I know, but maybe by the time we get there you can force down a piece of pepperoni pizza."

"I'm a vegetarian."

"Cheese pizza?"

She sighed.

Marcus turned forward again and stared out the window. Why had she wanted to get to know him if she wasn't willing to make an effort? He tried to recall what it was like to be thirteen years old. He had some hazy memories of teenage angst and raging hormones, but nothing to anchor him to Izzy's reality.

Especially not after what she'd been through. His own childhood might have been a little chaotic compared to most, but he'd had both of his parents, and he'd always been secure in their love for him. Izzy, on the other hand, had lost her mother and only just met her father today.

Maybe she was worried about losing him, too. Maybe it was easier to reject him first rather than risk being rejected.

He didn't know how she felt, but Ginger might. That had been his primary reason for asking her if they could spend the summer with her. She'd lost her parents as a child. She'd walked the same sad path Izzy was walking now, and maybe she could guide the girl through it.

Maybe she could guide him, too.

Of all the people he'd ever known, Ginger was the only friend he had who might be qualified to help.

And the fact that she was willing…

He owed her the sun and the moon for that.

CHAPTER FIVE

ONE AWKWARD LUNCH AND two even more awkward hours of driving went by before Ginger pulled into the driveway of her Promise Lake house and killed the engine.

"Here we are," she chirped too brightly.

She had the distinct feeling everyone in the car was regretting having agreed to make this trip, and now here they were, about to shack up in her house as if they wanted to be together.

She'd made a horrible, terrible mistake. She didn't know Marcus anymore. She'd been a fool to think she could just invite him back into her life and everything would work out.

"This place is beautiful," Marcus said as they got out of the car. "How'd you find it?"

"Do you remember Soleil Freeman from college?"

He frowned. "I don't think so."

"She's the poet Anne Bishop's daughter?"

"Oh, right."

"Anyway, she went to school with us, and we've kept in touch over the years. I came here to visit the nonprofit farm she runs on the other side of the lake. She mentioned that she'd heard the local community college was looking for a writing instructor and, I don't know, things started falling into place. I got the job, and then soon as I saw this place I fell in love with it."

She popped the trunk and grabbed Isabel's bags. The girl had her hands full of dog and purse, so Ginger smiled and said, "Let me show you where your room is."

Izzy simply stared back, expressionless, then followed Ginger toward the front door. The girl was definitely depressed, Ginger decided, and she had every right to be, but it didn't make the situation any easier.

Ginger had been nine when she'd lost her own parents, and she remembered the listless, strange year afterward as if it was a bad dream she couldn't quite wake up from.

As she mused about how best to help the girl, Izzy let out a yelp from behind her.

"What is *that?*" she screeched.

Ginger turned and followed the direction of the

girl's gaze to the ground, where a fat slug was making its way across the porch.

"Banana slug," Ginger said. "They're harmless."

Izzy made a face. "They're disgusting."

"That, too."

"Are there many of them?" she asked.

"Nope. I've never seen one here on the porch. It must have lost its way in the woods. Oh, by the way," Ginger added, "there's quite a lot of wild-life around here. We'll have to keep a close eye on Lulu."

"What do you mean?"

"I just mean, you know, with hawks and coy-otes around…"

Oh God, had she ever picked a bad topic.

Izzy hugged the dog closer and continued to glare down at the slug as if it might make a sudden attack.

Ginger felt like pointing out that they were sur-rounded by icky, slimy, unpredictable nature and the girl had better get used to it, but she figured she wasn't going to win any points with that kind of talk, so she kept her mouth shut.

Izzy deserved her sympathy, not her sarcasm. Besides, Ginger remembered exactly how awful it felt to be thirteen. She could only imagine how painful it would be to lose you mother at such a volatile age. Nine had been bad enough.

The girl had gone through hell, and Ginger vowed not to add any more grief to her life, no matter how crappy Izzy's attitude got.

Once they were inside, she led Izzy down the hallway, giving a quick tour as they passed the living room on the right and the bathroom on the left. "Down the hall is the kitchen and dining room," Ginger said. "And this will be your room."

She turned on the light in the smaller guest bedroom. Its pale lilac walls gave the room a soothing feel that made Ginger consider painting her own room the same color. The guest room was furnished simply with an antique white wrought-iron bed, a weathered white dresser and a cheval mirror.

"You'll share the hallway bath with Marcus. I've set aside some extra towels in the bathroom—the pink set is yours."

The girl stared vacantly at the suitcases Ginger set down next to the dresser.

"I'm going to take Lulu out to do her business," she said. "Is there a place to walk around here?"

"You could take the path through the woods to the lake."

Izzy said nothing.

"Just go out the front door and around the house and you'll see the path." Ginger pointed east as she spoke. "It's a short walk."

The girl pulled a leash out of her purse and headed for the door, the dog still in her arms. Ginger followed her out to the living room, where she found Marcus studying photos on the fireplace mantel. There was a shot of Ginger's parents, one of Ginger with her grandmother, and one of Granny Townsend when she was a young girl.

He started to say something to Izzy, but she was through the door before he could get a word out.

"She's taking the dog for a walk," Ginger explained.

Marcus gave her a look that reflected a mixture of frustration and sympathy. He didn't need to say a thing. She knew exactly how he felt—or at least she could take a good guess.

It was surreal to have him standing in her living room, larger than life, studying her family photos. He was in so many ways her fantasy come to life. But, she had to remind herself, the fantasy and the reality had never met up before. And he was here as a friend now, one who'd nearly lost his life. But he was safe and in one piece. That was what truly mattered.

The moment he'd asked her if she would have

room for two houseguests, she'd know she was going to say yes. She definitely wanted to help Izzy and Marcus, but just as much, she wanted to help herself move on.

"Your room is behind the kitchen. Can I show you?"

"That's okay. I already figured it out and put my bags in there."

"Would it be good if I got lost for a while tonight, so you and Izzy can have some alone time?"

He grimaced. "I'm not sure either of us wants that right now."

"It might relieve a bit of the pressure to have one less person in the mix."

"Maybe." He gave the matter some thought as he turned away from the mantel and strolled to the French doors that looked out on the deck and the backyard and, beyond that, the woods and lake.

He peered out the door into the fading light of late afternoon and changed the subject. "Do you think she'll be okay out there alone?"

"Sure. The worst she might encounter is an overgrown banana slug."

"No snakes? Scorpions? Hungry mountain lions?"

Ginger laughed. "Doubtful."

"I never took you for a back-to-the-woods kind

of girl. I thought you'd live out your life in the urban jungle."

Ginger sighed. "I guess the urban jungle wore me down."

"What do you mean?"

She shrugged, unsure herself what she meant. But then she opened her mouth and out came words she knew were true.

"I couldn't spend any more time being perpetually single and living in an apartment and feeling like something was missing."

"So you figured out that redwood trees were missing?" he joked.

She crossed the living room and opened the double doors onto the deck so that the early evening breeze could flow through the house. "I needed to get out of the city, and this place cast a spell on me. Well, it and Soleil's baby girl," she added, only half joking.

Ginger felt a little shy talking about the main reason she'd moved here.

"Oh?"

"I knew when I met Soleil's baby that I wanted to have a child of my own. I mean, I knew it before, but when I held her little girl, I felt the wanting somewhere deep down, you know?"

Silly question. Of course he didn't know.

"So your biological clock's ticking, huh?" He flashed a wry grin that somehow annoyed her.

"That reduces what I felt to a cliché, and it didn't feel like a cliché."

He sobered. "I'm sorry. It must be hard, wanting a baby and not being able to afford one." He added this last part as if it didn't compute.

And truly, it was an odd dilemma when she thought of his own problem—accidentally having a child he'd never thought he wanted.

Ginger shrugged. "It's an abstract problem at the moment. I've just been dealing with the more tangible problem of getting this house repaired, and the more I try to fix, the more I find wrong."

He smiled. "It's great to see you doing so well."

His tone was warm, but… But that's all it was. There wasn't any interest on Marcus's part about whether she had a boyfriend or a lover or anything else. Otherwise he would have asked by now. She'd known there wouldn't be, but given that the last time they'd seen each other she'd still been pining after him, she supposed old habits were hard to break.

This was good. She'd moved on in her heart, and now her subconscious was catching up to it. This was exactly why she needed to spend time with Marcus, so she could prove to herself that what she'd had with him was a lasting friendship, not a missed romance.

She was older now, more mature. She knew better than to get caught up in those old romantic feelings again, that misguided longing.

"So what about the man situation? Anyone special in your life?"

Okay. He was interested.

"Special?" she repeated.

His smile turned playful. "You know what I mean."

"No one," she said, shrugging.

She hoped she sounded casual, but she feared the truth had slipped into her voice. She didn't want him to know that she'd spent well over a decade finding out that one guy after another didn't measure up to her standards—standards that she'd based on him.

How could she have let so many years slip past her with such unrealistic expectations?

"So what about this guy you almost married. Who was he?"

"Can I get you a drink?" Ginger said, dodging the question. "Glass of wine, maybe?"

"That sounds great."

She led him into the kitchen, then retrieved a decent bottle of cabernet from the wine rack on the counter. "I was thinking of making a little spa-ghetti carbonara for dinner, but since Izzy's a vegetarian…"

"I'm sorry. It doesn't look like she's going to make anything easy." He pulled out a chair and took a seat at the breakfast table.

"It's okay. She's thirteen. She's just doing what she's supposed to do."

"She's supposed to drive everyone crazy?"

"She's supposed to start asserting her indepen-dence."

His shoulders sagged. "I'm so unequipped to handle this."

"I was thinking… There's a really good therapist in town. Maybe it would help to get Izzy into therapy with her. Or maybe both of you?"

"That's a great idea."

Ginger removed the cork and smelled it, savoring the spicy, oak-tinged scent of fermented grapes. She turned just in time to catch an odd expression crossing Marcus's face as he watched her. But as soon as their gazes met, the expression vanished.

"I'll find her card and give it to you."

"Do I get to hear the story of 'almost'?" he asked, grinning again.

"Oh." She shrugged as she retrieved glasses from

the cupboard. "I guess so. But first, how does pasta primavera sound? I think I've got enough vegetables to throw a decent dinner together."

"Perfect. Thank you so much for thinking of Izzy. I'll take her for a grocery shopping trip first thing tomorrow to make feeding her easier."

Ginger poured them each a glass of wine and brought Marcus's to the table.

"Cheers," she said, toasting. "To new beginnings."

"Cheers—to *you*," he said, and something in his eyes set her insides tingling.

It was almost as if he was looking at her flirtatiously, but that was the old Ginger thinking. The new Ginger knew better. The new Ginger was going to learn from the past and remember that there wasn't any reason to take Marcus's warmth or his gaze or his anything else as a sign of romantic interest. He'd already proved himself incapable of seeing her as a desirable woman.

Right?

Right.

She just had to figure out how to get all the warm tingly stuff to stop happening, since he was still the same ridiculously attractive man he'd always been.

She took a drink of wine and allowed the sharp

burst of flavor to distract her. Savoring the notes of plum, blackberry and spice gave her a few moments to decide how to explain her almost marriage.

"I was with Leo for eight years," she finally said as she set her glass on the counter and began rummaging around for dinner ingredients.

"Leo? You almost married a guy named *Leo?*" His teasing tone caused Ginger to smile, but she didn't give him the satisfaction of seeing it.

"It was short for Leonardo, if you must know. He was Italian."

"Why didn't you want to marry him?"

Because of you was definitely not the appropriate response at the moment. Nor was it entirely true. "I…don't know. He was great," she said, shrugging.

He just wasn't you.

No, she had to stop thinking that way. She knew she'd been unable to marry Leo because she believed there had to be a guy out there who could make her feel the way Marcus had once made her feel—only this time the guy would actually return her interest.

She filled a pot with water for the pasta.

"I get it. You weren't ready. Believe me, I know how that feels."

There was no point correcting him. "The breakup

was inevitable. I can see now that I look back on it. I'm not sure my heart was ever really into it."

"If your heart wasn't there, where was it?"

This was the kind of poetically poignant question that had made Ginger fall for Marcus so many years ago. He saw right to the heart of things—well, most things and most people. But not her. He'd never quite seen her heart.

She sighed, willing herself once again not to blurt out any uncomfortable truths. "I don't know. I guess my heart was in hiding. Afraid of committing or whatever."

He laughed. "You? Afraid of commitment? That's supposed to be my line."

"Why are you the only one who gets to use it? How many committed relationships did you ever see *me* in?"

"There was that one guy—what was his name? Neddy?"

"Teddy."

She cast a glance at Marcus over her shoulder and caught him grinning wickedly.

"Right," he said. "You were with him for what? A year?"

"Yeah, something like that."

"But it doesn't matter how many relationships I

saw you in. The point is I know what kind of person you are. You're not afraid of intimacy. You're probably devoted to it more than anyone I've ever known."

"I am not," Ginger protested, but as the words left her mouth, she realized he was right.

She was devoted to the idea of intimacy, and she'd done a great job of finding it with her friends. It was in her romantic relationships that she'd fallen short. And maybe it was her devotion to some ideal intimate relationship that had tripped her up.

An ideal intimate relationship with the one guy she'd ever loved, the one sitting at her kitchen table. A man she now wanted only to be friends with.

But the mere fact that he knew her so well sent the unwanted tingly sensations in her belly into overdrive. Her grip slipped from the heavy pot of water, sending it clattering into the sink.

"Need any help there?" Marcus called as she cursed and began filling the pot again.

"No, thanks."

"So you're still thinking about adopting, even without the guy around?"

"I don't know. It would be a long shot. But I'm getting older, and I don't want to put off having a child until some man I might never find comes along, you know?"

"Of course you'll find the right guy if you really want to." There was firm conviction in his voice.

"You make it sound so easy."

"Look at yourself." Marcus sounded incredulous now.

She turned to him to make sure she hadn't misread his tone. "What do you mean?"

"You're amazing—beautiful, smart, funny, accomplished. What guy wouldn't want to be with you?"

What guy, indeed?

She bit her tongue. *Not now.* Not now.

This wasn't the time to castrate him verbally for his utter and complete inability to see why she'd managed to be a failure with men all these years.

But the fact that he'd called her beautiful…

That sent the warm tingly storm south, into dangerous territory.

Pathetic.

She was completely hopeless if this was how she responded to a mere compliment from the guy she was supposed to be over.

She knew she was an attractive woman. Over the years she'd shed the insecurity of her twenties, along with the extra fifty pounds she'd managed to carry around from her preteen years, and she liked who she was and how she looked. She wasn't perfect, but she was comfortable in her body.

So why did Marcus's approval make her feel so damn fluttery?

Old habits, perhaps.

Or maybe it was just that he was finally giving her a compliment she'd deeply craved once upon a time.

"Isn't the real problem finding a guy that *I* want to be with?" she said at last.

"Ah, good point."

Ginger poured olive oil into a pan, turned the burner on low, then began crushing garlic to add to it. "So what about you?" she said as she worked.

"I'm definitely not looking for the right guy."

"You know what I mean."

"I was dating someone. Long distance. You know me. Love to put a country or even a continent between me and my beloved. But we called it quits when I decided to move back here."

"Who is she?"

"Her name is Annika. She's Dutch. I met her in Amsterdam, but she traveled a lot for work. I saw her whenever she was in town, which was rarely."

Ginger couldn't help herself. "Just the way you like it?"

"I thought so. But when I was lying in the hospital after the shooting and the nurse asked me who I'd like her to contact about what had happened…"

His voice had changed before he trailed off. He'd sounded uncertain, or maybe unsettled.

Ginger dumped a handful of crushed garlic into the oil and turned to look at him. But his expression was inscrutable.

She began chopping vegetables as he continued.

"I realized there wasn't anyone it mattered all that much to contact."

"I'm sure your girlfriend cared that you were shot."

"Yeah, but we didn't really stay in touch when she was out of town. I knew she was off somewhere working on a story, and…I don't know. I guess it was the first time I realized she and I were actually more like friends with benefits than significant others."

"And you don't call your friends with benefits from the hospital after an emergency."

"Right."

"So who did you call?"

"No one."

Again she turned, just in time to catch the haunted look in his eye.

"I'm sorry, Marcus. It makes me wish we'd stayed more in touch, you know? I wish I could have been there."

"No worries. I was happy to get your message when I returned to Amsterdam."

"Is that when you heard from Izzy, too?"

"Yeah. She said something like, 'Hi, uh, this is, uh…Isabel Grayson. Uh, I'm Lisette Grayson's daughter. And, uh, you're my dad.'"

"I can't believe you have a kid. You, of all people…" Ginger shook her head, then glanced over her shoulder to smile at him. But her smile vanished when she saw the uncertainty in his eyes.

And for the first time, she glimpsed how he really felt about having a thirteen-year-old girl take over his life.

He was more than just afraid. He was lost. Wandering a planet he'd never visited before, somewhere on the opposite side of the universe.

CHAPTER SIX

ONCE THEY'D MADE IT through a semi-pleasant dinner and Izzy had gone off to bed for the night, Marcus suggested they take their third glass of wine and go for a walk around the property.

He could hardly believe how settled Ginger's life seemed. How grown up she was. Which was foolish. Of course she hadn't remained frozen in time as a twenty-one-year-old college student. Of course she'd moved on to become someone more than the girl he'd once known.

But what surprised him most was how appealing he found this mature Ginger. She wasn't as remote or sophisticated as the women he usually went for. She'd always been a warm, welcoming person, but it had been her sense of humor and her take on life that had made her his best friend. That part of her hadn't changed, and yet, somehow she was transformed.

"I'm hoping to revive this rose garden someday,"

she said, gesturing to a row of forlorn-looking rose bushes along the side of the house. "The previous owners were gardeners."

"I remember you having a bit of a green thumb back in the day."

"That one little window box outside my dorm window didn't really count as a garden."

"You grew basil."

She laughed. "Yeah, I still do. Anything I can eat, I grow. I'm just not good with flowers, but I'm going to get there."

They rounded the side of the house, and Marcus spotted a couple of raised beds filled with healthy-looking plants. "Ah, see? I know you better than you think I do."

She beamed as she knelt next to one box and lovingly propped a vine back against its supporting stick.

"Are those tomatoes?"

"Sugar snap peas. The heirloom tomatoes are over there."

"Wow." In truth, he didn't know much about growing vegetables.

He just knew that the sort of constancy and stability required to garden had never been his thing. Those very qualities had been part of what had attracted him to Ginger—and at the same time made him wary. That constancy also made her a great friend, but now that he was seeing her in her new confident and curvaceous glory, he realized that she was just the kind of loyal, reliable woman he was terrified of.

She was supposed to be the one woman he could be friends with without ever having to worry about sex coming between them.

But here she was now, a whole new woman. The same, but irresistibly different.

Give him emotionally unavailable women on different continents any day. He knew how to handle them. They were safe.

"I've been wondering," she said, "how are you doing since the shooting?"

"I'm healed up fine," he answered.

"No, I mean, how are you *doing?*" she asked as they continued along the path toward the woods.

"It's weird—ever since getting on the plane to come back here, I feel like the shooting didn't even happen to me. It's like it happened to someone else."

"Because you feel safer here?"

"I guess so. And maybe it's partly that I've been so preoccupied thinking about Izzy, I don't have time to worry about anything else."

"Now you have to keep yourself alive not just for yourself, but for her, too."

He winced. "Gee, thanks for reminding me."

"Anytime," she joked, but he knew she was right.

He had a huge responsibility now. He was a father. Impossible, but true.

"I guess it's the classic near-death-experience reaction," he said, knowing Ginger wouldn't laugh at him, "but I've had this sense that I'm supposed to drastically change my life somehow, ever since I first woke up in the hospital."

"You're supposed to make right all your wrongs?"

"Yeah, me and Ebenezer Scrooge. Actually, it's more like I want to experience things I haven't experienced before. I'm thirty-six years old, you know, and there's a lot I haven't done yet."

"Like what?"

They paused at a bench that looked out on the lake. Sitting up on a bluff, beneath some trees, it provided an expansive view. Ginger sat down, and Marcus followed suit.

"Like…I don't know. Be a father?"

"Box number one, check."

He chuckled. "Yeah, didn't even have to work at that one. It just fell into my lap."

"What else?"

"Um, you know, maybe settle down a bit?"

Ginger cast a shocked look at him. "Get out."

"No, really."

"I guess that sort of goes hand in hand with being a dad," she suggested.

"Well, I could do it the nomadic way, like my parents did, but I want Izzy to have a better life than I did."

"You sound as if you've given this some thought."

"Not really," he joked. "It's just that the wine is going to my head."

But that was only half-true.

He was having thoughts he'd never had before. He'd taken one look at Ginger's beautiful, decrepit cottage and felt for the first time that he wanted a home of his own. Not a place where he lived for a short time, but a real home, where he could put down roots and grow a life for himself and Izzy, and maybe someone else, too. Izzy would need a woman in her life someday, and so did he. Hell, he wanted to do the family thing all the way—get married, raise kids, take the hand Fate had dealt him, and play it through.

He hardly recognized the crazy thoughts he was having. But he felt so present, so thankful to be alive, that he wanted to run with each wild idea.

For instance, what would it be like to kiss Ginger?

Was she a good kisser? He had no idea. Was she warm and eager or cool and reserved?

He was hoping for the former as he stared at her mouth.

"The thing about a near-death experience," he said, "is that it makes you wonder what you're missing out on. It makes you want to live in the moment more, and do whatever the hell you feel like doing."

She looked at him curiously, her eyes luminous in the fading light. "Oh, yeah? What else do you think you've been missing out on?"

"You," he said.

He hadn't meant to say it, but he *had* drunk half a bottle of wine.

And it was true. Sitting here right now, he couldn't think of anything on earth he was more curious to experience than Ginger.

He slid closer, leaned in and placed a gentle kiss on her lips.

No sooner did he wonder how she was going to react than he felt her response. She was, as he'd hoped, warm and eager. After the initial shock, she kissed him back, her soft, pliant lips coaxing his into a deeper kiss.

Wow.

He pulled back a bit, looked her in the eyes and

smiled slightly. "That was nice," he said. "Can we do that again?"

The words were barely out of his mouth before she parted her lips, and he leaned in again. This time he lingered, explored, tasted.

His body responded with an eagerness the likes of which he couldn't recall having felt before. He shifted closer and put one palm on her waist. He was contemplating where it might go next when Ginger's own hand landed on top of his.

She stiffened and pulled back from the kiss.

"What's wrong?"

She sighed. "Where did that come from?"

He grinned. "My near-death experience? Carpe diem, right?"

"Seriously. I…we…we're friends. How would Izzy feel if she saw us out here like this?"

Right. Izzy. He was supposed to be thinking of her needs first.

The thought sobered him, and he slid back until a proper twenty-four inches separated them.

"Sorry," he said. "I'm still getting used to this thinking-of-the-kid-first stuff."

"Yeah, well, I just don't want to screw up the summer before it's even gotten started."

"Right, right, good thinking."

"And seriously. What on earth is going on, Marcus? You've never showed the slightest romantic interest in me before."

He sighed and ran a hand through his hair. "Yeah, yeah, I know. We're friends, and I don't want to mess that up. I've always wanted to protect our friendship."

It was a lame excuse in a way. Because of course he'd never thought of kissing her back in college. They'd both had to grow up for him to see Ginger's appeal. Now he was looking at her through the eyes of a grown man—and a father—rather than the selfish perspective of a guy on the run from everything and everyone.

"I know you're going through tough times, and maybe it's tempting to seek the closest—and most convenient—comfort."

"Right," he said. "I guess you're right."

It was true, he supposed. The comfort of a willing woman's arms sounded like a welcome distraction right now. Too bad that woman couldn't be Ginger.

MARCUS'S GREEN EYES WERE barely visible in the moonlight. The two of them paused at the back door of the house, both reluctant to go inside, to leave behind this crisp, quiet night and whatever crazy spell it had cast over them a few minutes ago. As Ginger looked at him, trying to think what to say, only one subject came to mind.

That kiss...

Dear God. Ginger was going to spend the rest of her sad little life replaying that kiss in her head. Wishing she'd said or done something different.

Wishing she'd had the guts to go for it even though she'd known it was wrong.

"I'm really sorry," Marcus began. "I didn't mean to make things awkward—"

She held up a hand to stop him. "Don't mention it. How about we just pretend it never happened?"

He shrugged, then nodded. But his gaze searched hers for something else.

Was he trying to decide if she meant what she said?

"I was thinking," he finally said. "You mentioned your house needs some work, right?"

"Yes."

"I'm a little rusty, but as you might remember from my summer jobs, I know my way around a construction site pretty well."

"Oh," she said, blinking in surprise at the idea.

"How about I repay your generosity in letting us stay here with my carpentry services?"

"I don't know." This was the last thing she'd

expected him to throw at her. "You'll need to be spending time with Izzy, getting her settled, getting to know her—"

"Sure, but I'll drive her crazy if I'm hovering around her constantly. She needs space, too."

Ginger gave the matter some thought. She couldn't afford to hire a contractor anyway, so in truth, she was thrilled at the prospect of free labor.

"Wow," she finally said. "I have to admit, I love the idea."

He smiled. "Great. I'll get started in the next day or so. We can talk about your priority list tomorrow and what needs to be done."

They said good-night, and Ginger went to her room, closed the door and flopped down on the bed, her body still buzzing with so much adrenaline from their kiss that she wasn't sure she'd ever be able to fall asleep.

She buried her face in her pillow and let out one of those silent screams her therapist had taught her to use when she was frustrated and in a place where real screaming would be inappropriate. It didn't help, though. She still wanted to scream out loud.

Flipping onto on her back, she did an inventory of all her tingling body parts and decided there wasn't any use denying it—she was in for a long, sleepless, lonely night.

But Ginger was no stranger to insomnia. She'd suffered from it on and off since her parents' deaths, and she got some of her best writing done in those long, sleepless nights. In a sick way, she almost looked forward to bouts of insomnia.

She rose from the bed, grabbed the laptop computer she kept on her nightstand for just such occasions as this, and climbed back under the covers. As the screen started to glow, her mind began to settle into the quiet rhythm of composition. She'd learned years ago at writer's workshops in Iowa that writing, for her, was a form of salvation. It wasn't about the glory or egotism of publication. It wasn't about the need to make her voice heard. It was about saving herself from her own demons.

No, that made it sound more negative than it really was. More than anything, writing brought her joy. And a sense of peace that nothing else did. Lately, she'd been writing quiet little short stories about quiet characters making their way through quiet lives.

She didn't write so much for others as she did for herself. Which partly explained why Marcus was the famous author and she was happy teaching at the local community college.

As Ginger opened up the document that held her latest work in progress, she found herself unable to concentrate. Instead, her thoughts kept returning to Marcus, to what he'd said about changing, wanting to settle down, and to that completely unexpected kiss. How was she to feel about any of it?

Marcus had just survived a near-death experience, and clearly that colored his actions now. Was he serious about settling down, or was it just his fear of death propelling him into a frenzy of change that he'd later regret?

She suspected the latter was true, and she would have to be vigilant against getting sucked into something they'd both later regret.

But what about that kiss…

What if he didn't regret it? What if he wanted to see where it led? What if she did? What if the two people they'd become as adults had a chance to explore a relationship that they'd never had in their younger days?

Such questions were far too dangerous for her heart to contemplate, so she forced herself to begin typing.

CHAPTER SEVEN

MARCUS WOKE UP THE next day with a slight headache from the wine, wondering if the kiss could have worked out differently. He didn't regret it, exactly, but did regret having made Ginger feel uncomfortable. Of course she would worry about his motives in pursuing her romantically. Here he was, a new dad, just back in the U.S. after having been shot, and he was throwing himself at her after a matter of hours?

He must have seemed like a lunatic. And maybe he was, but he also knew from experience that life wasn't going to stop and wait for him. He had to seize his opportunities. Maybe he would just have to bide his time and prove to Ginger that he wasn't acting out of desperation to find a mother for his kid. Instead, he was a new man, and what he felt was a growing attraction to a woman he'd always considered a friend.

The house was silent as he rose and went about his morning routine. It was only when he walked down the hallway toward the kitchen that he heard the faint click clack of fingers typing on a keyboard. He followed the sound to the door at the end of the hall and found Ginger there, sitting at a desk.

"Morning," he said. "How long have you been up?"

She turned in the swiveling desk chair and smiled. "Oh, all night pretty much. I had trouble sleeping, and I eventually decided to spend my time writing instead of tossing and turning."

She was already dressed for the day in a pair of jeans and a stretchy pink tank top that created a warm glow on her pale skin, contrasting with her dark red hair. She was so damn pretty. He forced his gaze from lingering on the rounded swell of her breasts, and looked around the office.

"I hope I wasn't the cause of your sleeplessness."

"Don't give yourself so much credit," she said in a teasing tone. "If you'll remember, I've always had insomnia."

"Oh, right." He entered the room, perusing the bookshelves that lined the walls. "So this is where you write."

"Sometimes. I have a laptop for when I want to be more mobile."

"What are you working on these days?"

"Nothing much."

"Nothing much that kept you up all night?"

She laughed. "Yeah, okay, it's a short story, but I'm not going to let you read it."

He spun around, assuming an expression of mock offense. "How can you not let me read it? You're the best writer I know and I used to be your favorite critic."

"False flattery will get you nowhere—and you haven't read anything of mine in years."

"Seriously, Ginger, that short story you wrote about the girl lost in the desert still gives me chills."

Ginger rolled her eyes and groaned. "Oh God, you remember that thing?"

"I still have a copy of it. I found it while I was packing for my trip here."

She pointed her finger at him. "Use it for kindling next time you need to start a fire."

"You should write a novel."

"Everyone who writes novels thinks I should stop wasting my time with short stories, and write a novel."

Marcus leaned against her desk, wanting very much to read what she had on the computer monitor. She minimized the document to keep him from doing so.

"So why don't you?" he said.

"If you'd stayed in touch, you'd know that I did write one, and it was an utter failure."

A stab of well-deserved guilt shot through him. "I'm sorry. But sales have little to do with talent. I want to read your book. I bet it's great."

"It's over there on a shelf somewhere. Help yourself."

"So why not write another one?"

"I'll leave the wordy tomes for talented writers like yourself."

"How about a book of short stories then?"

Ginger crossed her arms over her chest and peering up at him. "Is there some reason you're so interested in my writing efforts?"

He loved the intelligent, feisty spark in her eyes.

"Because it's a lot easier than thinking about my own writing?"

She laughed. "Fair enough."

He stood up and went to the bookshelves, scanning until his gaze landed on a book spine that bore the name Ginger Townsend.

"*Spells for Lost Girls,*" he said, reading the title aloud.

"It's actually based on that short story about the girl in the desert."

He pulled the book off the shelf, his chest swelling with pride. He'd known that story was outstanding. He'd always told her so.

"Wow," he said. "I'm impressed."

"Don't be. It sold about five copies."

He quickly flipped pages to chapter one, eager to read the opening lines.

"Oh God," she said. "Don't read it in front of me."

"Okay, okay."

He closed the book and found himself staring at the back cover, which displayed a black-and-white photo of Ginger leaning against a brick wall, her wild, curly hair draped over her shoulders in all its glory, her face wearing a far-off, mysterious expression that was somewhere between knowing and searching. She didn't look into the camera, but rather into the distance to some dreamy place where no one could reach her.

"Just tell me you like it after you read it, whether you do or not," she said, and he knew she was quite serious. "I don't want any brutal honesty."

"Stop it. I know it's going to be brilliant, because you wrote it."

Her cheeks turned pinker, and she glanced down the hallway. "Izzy's still sleeping, I guess."

"I'll check on her. Can I get you something for breakfast?"

"I've already had some toast," she said, standing up. "Why don't I get you something?"

"No, it's fine. I'll—"

"I insist. You're the guest, and I'm sick of writing now."

"Thanks. I'll read your book tonight."

"I was thinking maybe I could show you guys around the area today. How does that sound?"

"I don't want you to go to any trouble."

"I'd love to. It's fun playing tour guide, and it'll help you both feel more independent if you know your way around."

"Okay, thanks. That sounds great." He stepped aside and followed her into the kitchen.

Gratitude for her generosity welled up, and he had to resist the urge to sweep her into his arms and kiss her again. Resisting went against his new philosophy to live life to its fullest, but he supposed a little self-restraint was in order at the moment.

How had he managed never to fall in love with this glorious woman before?

He went down the hall, forcing his thoughts away from Ginger, and stopped at Izzy's door. He knocked softly and heard the whimper of the dog from inside, then the scrape-scrape of little toenails on the floor. He eased the door open and let the dog out, then peered in at the lump in the bed with the mess of long dark hair.

"Izzy?" he called softly.

No answer.

He stepped inside and walked over to the bed as the dog took off down the hall toward the kitchen, probably in desperate need of a potty trip outside. Izzy's breathing didn't have the slow steadiness of deep sleep, so he sat down on the edge of her bed and waited for her to open her eyes. For the moment she didn't stir.

This girl he barely knew was depending on him to be the best father he could possibly be. Was he up to the task? He believed he was, and part of him was eager to prove he could be a good dad. But that made the responsibility no less daunting.

She was embarking on the teenage years, and the last time he'd known a teenage girl up close and personal...well, he'd been a teenager himself, doing things he couldn't imagine—and didn't want—this child ever doing. And part of her was still a child. That much was easy to see. She was straddling the easy innocence of childhood and the tumultuous issues of adolescence, with one foot more firmly in the latter.

She rolled over toward him and yawned. Her eyes fluttered open when her leg bumped against his hip.

"Morning, Izzy," he said.

"Um, hi."

"Did you sleep okay?"

"Yeah, I guess so. Where's Lulu?" she said, scanning the bed and the floor.

"Probably outside doing her business."

"What are you doing in here?" She sounded more curious than offended, and he was glad he'd made the effort to seek her out.

"I just thought I'd check in and see what you'd like for breakfast."

"Oh. Don't worry about me. I'm going to hang out in bed for a while and read maybe."

He was still holding Ginger's book. "That sounds nice, but Ginger wants to take us on a tour of the area."

"Oh."

"Did you know she's an author, too? This is her novel." He held it up for Izzy to see. "Maybe you can read it after I'm done with it."

Izzy frowned. "Isn't she your best friend? Why haven't you read her book before?"

"It, um..." Wasn't published in the Netherlands? Actually, he had no idea if it was, and he didn't want to lie. "I haven't been a very good friend," he admitted, vowing to change that.

"Why not?"

This whole honesty thing was going to be harder than he'd thought, and he had a feeling that Izzy and Ginger were going to push him for answers.

"It was just easier, I guess, living on the other side of the world." The excuse sounded lame even to him. "But I'm back now, and I'm going to make it up to her."

Izzy shifted and sat up. "I need to hit the ladies'. Do you mind?"

"I'll give you your privacy. We'll be leaving soon, so you'd better get dressed and come out to have a bite to eat, okay?"

"Yeah," she said, her voice flat.

Why had she been so eager to meet him and spend time with him, when she seemed so cool and disinterested now? It was weird.

Marcus left the room, went into his own bedroom and put the book on his bed for later. But he'd been honest when he'd told Ginger he wanted to read it. Suddenly too curious to wait, he sat on the edge of the bed and picked up the novel.

Ten pages later, he was utterly engrossed. Her writing was so beautiful, so lyrical, such a perfect expression of her personality on the page…. He wanted to stay there all day and finish the book. He recognized the main character as the desert girl from the short story she'd written in college, and everything that had been good about that story was in the novel, only more polished. Better.

Why was she not the darling of the literary world?

Well, he did know the business well enough not to ask such naive questions. Success had to do with so many factors out of the author's control... But still, she was a better writer than him, and he was going to insist she send her latest project to his literary agent.

"Marcus?" Ginger called from the doorway.

He looked up and grinned sheepishly.

"You're reading it already?" she said with a pained expression.

"How could I not? I love it. The first chapter is absolutely brilliant."

She rolled her eyes. "You're such a liar. Are you almost ready to go? Izzy's in the kitchen finishing a bowl of oatmeal."

"Oh, yeah. Thanks for feeding her. I'll be out in just a sec."

Alone again, he read the last page of the first chapter, and a warm glow washed over him. If this wasn't love, then he didn't know what was. If it was possible to fall in love with a woman through the words she'd written, then he'd just done it. But no, that wasn't entirely true. Because he already knew Ginger. He knew she was the best woman he'd ever met. He knew she was the personification of all the beauty she managed to create on the page.

Sure, falling for her could ruin their friendship, but not if she fell for him, too. He just had to figure out how to make it happen.

CHAPTER EIGHT

"It's just here, to the left," Ginger said, gesturing with her hand.

Marcus steered the Prius onto the gravel road marked by a sign that read Rainbow Farm. They'd made their way around the town of Promise, poking into the shops, stopping at a café for lunch and learning the whereabouts of all the key businesses. And they'd done a quick and dirty tour of the outlying areas around the lake, with Ginger pointing out trailheads and swimming spots along the way.

The area was breathtakingly pretty. It reminded Marcus a little of the commune in Oregon where he'd spent much of his childhood. The trees, the endless green… But the town of Promise felt stable and historic. It lacked the uneasy transience of commune life.

Now they were on their way to visit Ginger's friends Soleil and West.

"What is this place?" Izzy asked from the back-seat. She sounded suspicious. "You're not taking me to some back-to-nature program for bad teenagers, are you?"

Ginger made a little choked sound in her throat and shot a panicky glance at Marcus. "No!" she said, her voice too high. "This is my friend's farm. It's a really cool place I've been wanting to show you both."

"Oh." The response from the back of the car was unenthused.

"Well, I mean, actually, there *is* a program for teenagers here," Ginger amended as the car crunched along the gravel road through a wooded area. "It's an internship program for kids from Oakland. I thought you might enjoy meeting some other kids your age. You might want to hang out with them over the summer."

Izzy was silent. Marcus glanced in the rearview mirror and caught her expression.

"This is an organic farm, right?" he asked, to break the silence. "What do the kids do here?"

"I think they learn how to grow vegetables and take care of animals, so they can go back to the city and work in an urban garden project," Ginger explained.

"Why do they need to come all the way out here to learn that, if the project exists where they live?"

Ginger frowned. "I'm not sure. I think Soleil's background as a social worker has something to do with it. I'm sure she sees the program as more than just learning farming skills."

"You mean she counsels the kids, too?" Marcus asked, hoping Izzy didn't think that was the main reason they'd come out here.

"Not formally, I don't think. But I know she sees herself being a counselor above anything else."

They rounded a bend in the road and came into a clearing. Up ahead was a white Victorian farmhouse with a red roof, and spread out on rolling hills behind it was the farm itself.

"Beautiful, isn't it?" Ginger said.

"Yeah." Marcus took note of a group of kids playing a game of badminton off to one side of the garden. On the porch, a man stood overseeing a toddler unsteadily maneuvering her way down the front steps.

"That's Soleil's husband, West," Ginger said as if she'd read his mind. "And their daughter, Julianna."

"Are those *goats?*" Izzy asked, her tone vaguely horrified.

"Yep."

"Do I have to go in? I want to sit in the car."

Marcus turned around to look at her. "Don't be rude, Izzy," Marcus said.

Ginger peered at him, her expression inscrutable, then glanced back at Izzy herself. "You want to sit in the car? By yourself? For an hour?"

"Yes." There wasn't a lot of conviction in the girl's voice.

"Sure, go right ahead," Ginger said.

Marcus caught the doubt in Izzy's eyes as he glanced in the rearview mirror. She wasn't sure what kind of trap she was walking into.

"But I thought you wanted me to socialize or something?" she asked.

Ginger shrugged. "Not if you don't want to. I thought this would be fun for you, but if you're not interested, stay in the car."

He marveled at how calm and unbothered by Izzy's petulance she managed to be. He needed to figure out how to master that skill himself. It was part of the reason Izzy had seemed to respond so well to Ginger today as they toured the town, while she rebelled against Marcus's habit of always wanting to control the situation. How had he turned into an overbearing father figure so quickly?

He balked at the change in himself. While his own dad hadn't been a traditional father, with his radical politics and his laissez-faire approach to parenting, somehow Marcus had defaulted into the stereotype of a TV dad—his own *Father Knows Best* impersonation.

As they pulled to a stop in front of the house, the man on the porch swept the little girl into his arms and came toward the car to greet them. He was smiling tentatively, dodging the grabby hands of his daughter, who was trying to stick her fingers in his mouth.

Ginger and Marcus got out of the car, and she made introductions.

"How about the girl?" West asked, nodding toward Izzy, still sitting in the vehicle.

But before Marcus could explain his daughter's rudeness, she opened the door and got out as if nothing was the matter.

"This is my daughter, Izzy," he said, the words tripping awkwardly off his tongue.

It was his first time introducing her to anyone as his child.

"Hi," she said to West. "How old is your little girl?"

"Julianna's eight months old."

"And already walking—that's amazing," Ginger said.

"I don't think it counts as walking until she lets go of the death grip on my thumb, but yeah, she's a precocious one."

"Can I hold her?" Izzy asked. "I mean, do you think she'd mind?"

"She'll probably love it. She lives for attention." West handed the baby over to Izzy.

"She's so cute," Izzy cooed as she hefted the weight of the girl against her narrow hip.

"Don't let the cuteness fool you. The little demon never sleeps for more than two hours straight, and thinks flinging baby food is an Olympic sport and she's going for the gold." But his voice was softened by affection as he gazed at his daughter.

"Is Soleil around?" Ginger asked.

"Sure. You should come in. She'll be thrilled to see you."

"I should have called first, but we were driving by and I couldn't resist stopping in to show these guys the farm."

"Anytime you're always welcome," West said as they followed him up the steps and across the porch.

Inside, the house smelled of fresh-baked bread. Marcus looked around, admiring the gleaming hardwood floors and simple, unpretentious beauty of the place. It was much as he imagined Ginger's house would be once they got it fully renovated.

They?

Yeah, he was already imagining himself sticking around for the entire job…and beyond.

They followed West down a hallway to a large, eat-in kitchen, where a woman with a headful of springy black curls was explaining to a tall, gawky looking teenager how to properly slice bread.

"We've got some visitors," West announced.

The woman looked up, and a broad smile crossed her pretty face. "Ginger!"

The two hugged and turned to the group.

"You probably remember Marcus from college and this is his daughter, Izzy," Ginger said.

Soleil greeted them both, then gestured to the boy cutting the loaf of bread. "You guys are just in time to sample Omar's first effort at rosemary bread."

She introduced them to the youth, who looked to be maybe fifteen and was wearing a pink, flower-print apron over his baggy jeans and sports jersey. He grinned and said hello, and the smile transformed his dark brown face. Marcus watched as the boy's gaze landed on Izzy and lingered there, sparking with interest. Izzy, for her part, assumed a posture Marcus had never seen her take before, hair flipped over her shoulder, hip cocked to the side.

Okay, she was holding a baby, but there was no mistaking the change in her. She looked flirtatious.

As parenting challenges went, he wasn't remotely prepared for boys. His first instinct was to grab Izzy by the hand and drag her from the house, shuffle her back into the car and maybe drive her to the nearest nunnery.

She smiled a coy smile and said hello to Omar.

No, Marcus definitely wasn't prepared.

"Bread for everyone?" Soleil asked. "Omar, why don't you help me serve?"

"Ma!" the baby cried, reaching for her mother and trying to squirm out of Izzy's arms. "Mamamamama!"

"I could help with the bread," Izzy offered. "I think she wants you."

"Thank you, Izzy. She's probably getting hungry."

Marcus watched as his daughter went to the counter with Omar and began putting slices of bread on napkins.

"Why don't you give Marcus a tour of the place, West?" Soleil suggested as she sat down at the large oak kitchen table with Julianna squirming in her arms. "He's never been here before."

She casually flipped up her shirt and began nursing the baby, causing Marcus a moment's embarrassment. Not since his days on the commune had he been around the family scene, complete with breastfeeding moms and fussy toddlers. Suddenly, traipsing around a farm sounded like a marvelous idea.

"Izzy, why don't you come, too?" he said as she brought him and West slices of warm bread.

"Oh, um, I guess."

"Omar could show her around and introduce her to the other kids," Soleil said. "Would you mind, Omar?"

As he passed slices to Soleil and Ginger, he nodded. "Sure, that's cool." His eyes lit up and he smiled. "Hey, you want to see the chickens? We've got some crazy-looking ones."

Izzy, who'd taken a bite of her piece, shrugged. "Um, yeah," she said once she'd finished chewing.

"This bread is great," Ginger said.

"Delicious, Omar. I think you've found your calling," West added.

The boy smiled and motioned for Izzy to follow him. Marcus couldn't think of any good excuse to stop them. Okay, he was being an overprotective father. Surely there wasn't any harm in two kids taking a tour of the farm. Still, he made a mental note to keep an eye on them. After all, he was responsible for Izzy now.

"Come on out back," West said, motioning to Marcus. "I'll introduce you to the goats."

Marcus followed him reluctantly, hoping they'd quickly find their way around to the chicken coop. Chickens he was familiar with, but goats?

"So you're new to town, right?" West asked once they were crossing the yard behind the house.

A gorgeous Australian shepherd mix came running up to them and nudged Marcus's leg for attention. "Hey, buddy," Marcus said, bending to pet the dog.

"That's Silas. He'll make you stay there all day rubbing his head if you're not careful. So, you're here for the summer?"

Marcus straightened. "Yeah, I'm here for the summer. I'm, um, getting to know my daughter."

"Oh, right, Soleil mentioned that. You must have had quite a shock finding out you were a father."

Marcus smiled, surprised at himself. The topic didn't feel as weighty as it had even yesterday. His growing feelings for Izzy and Ginger, he suspected, were making him feel more positive about the situation.

"It was a shock at first," he said. "For Izzy, too, I'm sure. But we're adjusting. I guess the scariest part is the lack of a crash course in how to be a father. Any tips for a complete novice?"

They headed toward the pasture Silas following along behind.

"You know, I didn't find out about my daughter until Soleil was already five months pregnant. We had a rocky start, but things worked themselves out."

"And you're happy now?"

West smiled, and he didn't need to say a word. "Yeah. Being a father is hard, don't get me wrong, but it's amazing, too. Every single day is amazing, even the rough ones."

Marcus felt that now familiar stab of regret. "I wish I'd been around for Izzy's baby years."

"Is her mom still in the picture?"

"No, she died a few months ago."

"That's rough. I'm sorry."

"We hadn't been a couple since college." Marcus explained. "But it's rough for Izzy."

"It's good you've got Ginger around. I can't imagine a better role model for a teenage girl. You thinking of staying here in the area?"

Marcus hadn't been before he arrived, but now... "Maybe," he said. "I suspect we're going to like it here."

"I guess my only words of advice about the fatherhood thing is, you know, you've got to find it in yourself to be a better man than you ever thought you could be. Because your daughter doesn't deserve anything less."

Marcus chuckled. "That's what I was afraid of."

"You can do it, man, don't worry. If I can, anyone can."

But as Marcus surveyed this farm, the house, the barns, the animals, all the stability and responsibility it took to keep a place like this running, he wondered…. Was he way out of his element?

And even more important, was he cut out to be what Izzy needed?

Her happiness depended on the answer to that question.

He felt the euphoria of moments ago slipping away from him.

"I'm not sure I know what to do with a thirteen-year-old," he admitted.

"You'll figure it out. And she's welcome to come hang out with the kids here anytime you need a break. We'll teach her some useful skills—how to pluck a chicken and such."

Marcus laughed. "She's a vegetarian."

West grinned. "Then we'll teach her how to pick a cabbage. How's that?"

"I appreciate it," he said, not voicing his preference to keep her away from boys until the age of thirty.

"And don't sweat it," West continued, as if reading Marcus's mind. "Soleil runs this place with an iron fist in a velvet glove. You don't have to worry about the kids getting into any trouble."

"Has having a daughter given you any gray hair yet?" he asked West with a wry grin.

"I'm finding new ones every day."

CHAPTER NINE

GINGER WAS SOMEWHERE on the edge of a dream when she heard a knock at her bedroom door. Before she could react, the door creaked open.

"Ginger?" Marcus whispered.

"What wrong?" she croaked. "Is Izzy okay?"

"She's fine. Can I come in?"

"Um, yeah," she said, glancing at the clock on the nightstand. It was nearly midnight.

She sat up, leaned over and switched on a light, wondering for a brief moment of panic if her hair was a mess or if she had any dried-up drool on her chin.

Stop that. She wasn't the same foolish girl who'd pined after Marcus. She was a grown woman who understood that they'd never be more than friends.

"I'm sorry," he said. "I woke you up, didn't I?"

"Sort of."

He entered, filling up the room with his oversize

masculine form. It was the first time she'd had a man in this bedroom, she thought with a hint of regret.

"I just finished your book," he said, smiling as he sat down on the end of her bed and faced her. "I couldn't wait until morning to talk to you about it."

"Oh," she said, stunned. "You already finished it? I just gave it to you this morning."

"I've been reading it all evening. It's so damn good, Ginger. And I'm not just saying that. The way you wove the stories of the three girls together, and the spells. Brilliant. I really mean it."

She glanced away, uncomfortable with the effusive praise, even if he was just saying it to be nice.

"Are you sure you didn't crack your skull when you got shot? Suffer a brain injury, too?"

He shook his head, looking incredulous. "I'm serious, Ginger. I don't understand how that book went unnoticed, but it's one of the best things I've read in years. You should be very proud of yourself."

It wasn't like Marcus to gush. At least not the old Marcus. But this new guy who'd arrived on the plane from Amsterdam—she wasn't sure she knew all the rules when it came to him. He didn't behave in predictable ways. He didn't act like the guy she used to know.

"Thank you," she said. "I don't know what to say."

"Do you think you could get together some short stories for a collection? Something we could send to my agent?"

"No way! That's really nice of you, but—"

"Don't tell me you're not interested in publication anymore."

She shrugged, the movement making her conscious of how thin her blue silk nightgown was. One strap slipped off her shoulder and she grabbed it and put it back in place.

"I mean, of course I could use the money."

"Good. Then why don't I help you decide which stories to send?"

"Marcus…"

The prospect of letting him peruse her unpublished works left her feeling far more naked than the nightgown did. He knew her better than most people. Or at least she used to think. He knew which parts of a story were from her own life and which were made up. He could see through her fiction to her truths, and maybe that's why she was reluctant to have him read her work.

Or perhaps she was giving him too much credit.

"I can choose them myself," she finally said. "And then you can read them and see what you think."

"Tomorrow?"

"I don't know when I'll find time to look through everything. How many should I pick?"

He shrugged. "Just put together a few hundred pages worth. You don't have an agent now, do you?"

"No, we parted ways a few years after my book was published. She wasn't interested in representing short fiction."

"And you weren't interested in writing any more novels?"

"No."

"You really should. I mean, someday. When you're ready. The world needs your voice."

She sighed, trying not to laugh. "Don't you think you're laying it on a little thick? You don't have to say nice things to get me to let you stay here. I've already said yes, remember?"

He placed a hand on her leg, just below the knee, and the contact, even with a sheet between them, sent a shiver through her. "All kidding aside, okay?" He was gazing at her so earnestly she had no choice but to nod.

"Okay."

"I'm totally in love with your book. I'm going to let Izzy read it next, if that's fine with you."

"Oh. Wow. Do you think she's ready for it?"

Ginger had written the book as an adult novel,

even though the three main characters were teenagers throughout much of the story.

"I think reading it will be good for her, yeah."

"Okay, but just wait until I talk to her about it first."

The protagonist lost her parents at the beginning of the story, and while Ginger was reluctant to introduce the subject to Izzy, she knew it was one that needed to be dealt with.

She was all too aware of Marcus's proximity and an awkward silence fell between them. She caught his gaze straying to her chest, if she wasn't mistaken, and her treacherous body tingled in all the wrong—right—places.

"In the novel, what did you intend for the reader to think when you had Greta and Jane disappear?" he asked, his eyes intent.

Ginger could hardly believe Marcus was sitting here acting as thought her unnoticed little book was the most important literary work to come along since the Bible.

"It was the spell. It worked."

"That's what I thought." He smiled, apparently satisfied. "Hey, I'm sorry. I know I shouldn't have woken you. I was just so excited to finish the story and…"

"And what?"

"I'm not kidding. It's a beautiful book. Almost as beautiful as you."

With that, he stood up and headed for the door, leaving Ginger to ponder his words.

Just before he walked out, he turned and said good-night, and she murmured a faint reply.

As she switched off the light and tried to go back to sleep, she wondered again if this seemingly new attraction he had for her was the real Marcus talking or the heady aftermath of his near-death experience.

And what if it wasn't false? What if he meant it?

It didn't matter.

She wasn't a big enough fool to love him again.

GINGER INHALED THE pungent scent of redwood trees as she watched a hawk circling high overhead, silhouetted against the bright blue sky.

Where had Izzy gone? Down the path to the lake, most likely. She'd taken off to walk the dog, and that was generally the way they went. Three days since her and Marcus's arrival, and the girl already had a daily routine. She spent much of her time at the beach, sunning herself, swimming or just playing with the dog.

Ginger strolled past the grove of redwood trees,

past blackberry bushes heavy with ripe fruit, past the mighty oak that stretched its branches over most of her backyard, and down the sloped path toward the lake. Up ahead to the left, she could see Izzy sitting on the beach, Lulu prancing around her, begging for attention.

Izzy's attention was elsewhere, though. She was staring out at the lake, or maybe past it to the horizon, her expression dark. A gentle breeze caught her long, dark hair and sent it fanning out slightly over her shoulders. She wore a gray T-shirt stretched tight over her thin frame, with a pair of faded jeans and white flip-flops.

And she appeared not to notice Ginger's approach. When Ginger finally sat down beside her and Lulu focused all her efforts on getting the attention of her owner, Izzy responded by glancing at Ginger. It was easy to see that the girl had been crying. Her face was blotchy, her eyes red and still damp.

"What?" Izzy said as a greeting.

Ginger tried to remember what it felt like to be thirteen. All she could recall was the utter misery. Awkwardness, self-consciousness, lack of confidence... She hadn't truly recovered from those same afflictions until her late twenties or early thirties. But then, she hadn't been nearly as naturally graceful as Izzy.

"I've been wanting to talk to you," she said.

The girl exhaled, clearly not interested. Ginger gave Lulu a thorough tummy rub, and the little dog edged her way onto her lap, clearly in ecstasy over the attention.

"Did Marcus tell you why he thought I'd be a good person for you guys to stay with this summer?"

"No." There was no hint of interest in the single-word response.

Ginger had hoped for a friendlier start to their conversation. She'd hoped to ease into the things she wanted to say, cushioning them with kindness. But Izzy was having none of that, so she decided to get to the point.

"One reason he brought you here is that I lost my parents when I was a kid."

Izzy glanced over at her, her expression more hostile now. Then she looked away again, back to the horizon.

"I was nine when it happened." Ginger could tell the story now without getting knocked down by grief, but for years she couldn't speak about it.

For years she hadn't talked about it. She'd simply gone about her life, knowing that people whispered about her behind her back. She'd endured their pitying looks—reveled in them, at times—but on the rare occasions when she'd opened her mouth and tried to tell the story to some curious person who asked about her family, her throat would close up and she couldn't get a word out.

She didn't cry, though. People always seemed impressed by that, as if her stoicism was some kind of virtue. Actually, the opposite was true, she'd found out during therapy. She'd been unable to grieve for her parents as a kid because the loss had been too big.

It had taken a therapist to point out that the reason she couldn't get close to men romantically was because she hadn't grieved for her parents yet. And that had finally set her on the path to crying the river of tears she needed to release.

"You mean like they died or what?" Izzy finally asked, her voice barely audible above the lapping of the water against the shore.

"Yes, they died."

"How did it happen?" Again, the quiet voice, though this time it was slightly more audible.

"They were in a car accident. A drunk driver—a car full of teenagers on their way to a party after the prom. My parents had gone out for dinner and were on their way home, but they never arrived. I was woken up later by the babysitter and the police knocking on the door."

Ginger stared out at the horizon, too, her chest tight. She didn't usually go into any details when she told people this story, but she'd vowed to give Izzy as much detail as she wanted if it would help her.

"So, what happened to you? Did you have to go to a foster home or something?"

"My grandmother was still alive. She took me in and raised me."

Izzy sat silent for a while. Ginger focused on the little dog, who lay contentedly in the crook of her crossed legs. She stroked her light brown fur, paying special attention to her favorite spots behind the ears and at the base of her spine.

"I know this sounds weird, but…did you ever get mad at your parents?"

Ginger knew she had to tread carefully here. "For leaving me behind?" she asked.

"Yeah." Izzy sounded a little defensive, as if she were embarrassed now that she'd dared to ask the question.

"Sure," Ginger told her. "And then I'd feel guilty for getting mad, and then I'd hate myself."

"Yeah." Izzy gave a heavy sigh.

"That's normal, Izzy. It's totally normal. We

spend our whole childhood knowing it's our parents' job to take care of us, and it's hard to accept that they're not going to be around anymore to do it."

"It's stupid." Izzy sounded angry now. "It's not like my mom wanted to get cancer."

"No, she didn't. And she didn't want to leave you."

"But she never even thought of finding my dad for me before she died. That makes me mad, too."

It made Ginger mad, as well, but she would never tell Izzy that. "Maybe she did think of it, but figured he wouldn't be able to help."

Izzy rolled her eyes.

"How did Nina become your guardian?"

"She was my mom's best friend and my godmother. They thought since I knew her and grew up around her, I'd be okay with going to live with her."

"And were you?"

She shrugged. "I'm not okay with any of it."

Ginger wasn't quite sure what "any of it" referred to, exactly, but she didn't think now was the time to press for details. She would try another tack.

"It was brave of you to contact Marcus like you did."

"No, it wasn't," she said flatly.

"He's a good person," Ginger said, hoping to reassure her, "but it's going to take him a little time to learn how to be a father."

"Are you, like, his girlfriend or something?" There was an edge in Izzy's voice.

Ginger, inexplicably, felt her face flush. "No, it's like he told you—we're old friends from college."

Izzy studied her closely. "You don't look at him like he's just an old friend."

Ouch.

Ginger's first instinct was to deny, deny, deny, but she didn't want to lie to Izzy. The girl would see right through her, and they'd never establish any kind of trust.

"Well, however you think I look at him, all we've ever been is friends."

"You like him," she said, and this time it was a clear statement of fact. "And not just as a friend."

Ginger laughed. The last thing she wanted was hostile, manipulative Izzy going back Marcus to report that Ginger had a crush on him. But the teenager had managed to back her into a corner, and she didn't see any way out. "Why do you say that?" she asked in as neutral a tone as she could.

"I'm not stupid."

Ginger shrugged, giving in to defeat. After all,

hadn't she invited Marcus to stay with her in order to get over her old feelings for him?

Lulu, spotting a small bird nearby, jumped up from Ginger's lap and pranced over to investigate.

What was she about to say to Izzy was probably too mature for the girl to understand, but she had vowed to be honest with her.

"Okay, well, here's the deal," Ginger said. "I have a long history of going for emotionally unavailable men. My therapist says it's my way of not having to get too close to anyone. Self-sabotage, basically. I fear abandonment, since my parents abandoned me in a sense. So I fall for men who won't ever fall for *me,* since that means they'll never get close enough to leave me."

"What's self-sabotage?"

"It's when your subconscious—the part of your brain that you're not aware of—leads you to do things that are in conflict with what your conscious mind thinks it wants."

Izzy scrunched up her forehead. "That doesn't make any sense."

"No, it doesn't. I agree."

"I guess it's the same for me—like, how being mad at my mom for dying makes no sense."

Lulu barked at something in the woods, and

Ginger turned to see that the bird she'd been pursuing a few moments ago had perched on a nearby tree branch, frustrating the dog.

"We all want to feel there's someone to blame for the bad stuff that happens," Ginger said, relieved that the conversation had neatly traveled away from her feelings for Marcus, and equally relieved that she'd managed to both distract Izzy from her sadness and chip away at a bit of her hostility.

"So you like Marcus because he's emotionally unavailable? What does that mean?"

Okay, so she'd congratulated herself too soon. Ginger sighed.

"In your dad's case, it just means that he's always seen me as a friend, not a potential girlfriend."

"But people can go from being friends to boyfriend and girlfriend, can't they?"

Marcus's daughter was certainly persistent. "Sure, it happens."

"So why couldn't it happen with you two?"

Ginger wanted to tell Izzy it wasn't any of her business, but she was scared of ruining the little progress she'd made in gaining the girl's trust.

"Good question," she said vaguely.

The wind was starting to pick up. At this time of day, the change of temperature often caused a strong breeze to sweep across the lake and chase away those who, like Ginger and Izzy, hadn't brought a warm jacket along for the evening.

When Izzy shivered, Ginger took the opportunity to change the subject.

"Would you like to come back to the house and help me make dinner?" she asked.

"I don't like to cook."

"Really? Have you ever tried?"

The girl shrugged. "I've made eggs, but I burn them."

"Maybe what you need is a little instruction so you can enjoy the process."

For a moment Ginger was sure Izzy would refuse, but instead the girl stood up and caught Lulu in her arms to put her leash back on.

"I thought we could make a few pizzas. Sound good?"

"Whatever. So long as they're vegetarian."

They headed back toward the cottage in silence until they reached the oak tree.

"When your parents died," Izzy asked, "did you have nightmares?"

Ginger stopped walking. "Are you having insomnia?"

The girl nodded, staring down at the dirt path.

"I did. I had horrible nightmares, and I had a hard time sleeping."

She chose not to add that they'd gone on for years, that even in her twenties she'd slept with the lights on because she was so scared of what awaited her in her dreams. But she made a mental note to talk to Marcus about making an appointment for Izzy to see a therapist as soon as possible. Maybe she could prevent Izzy's grief from warping her life as much as Ginger's had warped hers.

"What kind of nightmares?" Izzy asked as they began walking toward the house again.

Lulu, sensing familiar territory, tugged against the leash and Izzy released it so the dog could run up onto the rear deck and wait at the door. She pranced there in excitement, brown eyes cast back at them in eager expectation of dinner.

"One of the most recurrent dreams was that I'd be crossing a bridge on foot," Ginger began. "Sometimes it would look like the Golden Gate Bridge, sometimes the Richmond Bridge, sometimes the Bay Bridge—but there wouldn't be much of a bridge to cross. There'd just be a few rickety boards on metal supports, and I could see the water down below, and every time I moved, one of the boards would feel like it was giving way and I'd almost fall."

"Oh."

They reached the back door, where the rickety screen reminded Ginger of yet another repair that needed to be made on her money-sink of a home, and went into the house. While Izzy fed the dog, Ginger got out the fixings for dinner.

She hadn't thought about those dreams in at least a few years. Relatively benign as they sounded when she described them, they'd always made her wake up with a scream caught in her throat, her body drenched in sweat.

In real life, she had no fear of bridges, but in her dreams they were objects of sheer terror. And when she thought of Izzy, her young life caught in that same cycle of sleepless hell, Ginger vowed she'd do whatever she could to make things easier for the girl.

CHAPTER TEN

IZZY CAUGHT ON TO chopping vegetables. She liked the fact that Ginger didn't fuss over her handling such a sharp knife. She'd simply showed her how to hold it safely, warned her to keep her fingers tucked away from the blade and taught her how to chop a green pepper.

Easy.

She worked her way through peppers and onions, and was now chopping mushrooms for the pizzas. She was happy that they didn't have to keep talking. Ginger had put on some kind of African music that made the house feel alive.

Izzy didn't really want to like Ginger. Most of the time she wanted the woman to go away, which didn't make much sense when she and Marcus were staying at *her* house. But she kind of liked Promise Lake.

She wondered if Marcus might consider getting them their own place here once the summer was over. Or would he want to go back to Amsterdam? Or somewhere totally different? She didn't want any more changes, and she was terrified of asking him the most important question—what came next?

What came after this getting-to-know-you vacation?

She liked the name Promise Lake. It sounded soothing, somehow.

Hopeful.

Full of good things to come.

That was how Izzy wanted to feel.

And she liked the sounds of the forest and the lake—they were somehow more like quiet than noise. The birds, the bugs, the frogs, the rustling of the trees that reminded her of breathing—it all worked its way inside her and made her feel calm in a way she hadn't felt in Nina's house in the city, where everything had seemed cold and mechanical.

Izzy even liked this broken-down house, with its crooked floors and crumbling walls. The light that poured through the big windows felt quiet and happy, and the bright, pretty colors Ginger had painted the walls made every room feel as if it were welcoming her to come in.

Most of all, she liked sleeping in what clearly had been meant to be a girl's room. Ginger had told her that she hoped to someday adopt a child. Some stupid, stupid part of her thought maybe Ginger wouldn't need to adopt a little girl from China if she got together with Marcus. Then Izzy would be—

No.

Stop it.

That was by far the stupidest thought that had ever tried to form in her head, and she wasn't going to go there. It was the kind of ridiculous fantasy some girl in a Disney movie would have—thinking everything would work out hunky-dory in the end and everyone would live happily-freaking-after…*blah blah blah.*

Like her mother had told her in one of their talks after the cancer had gotten bad, life never worked out like the fairy tales and Disney movies. Well, except in one way. The mom really did die sometimes.

But Izzy really, really didn't want to like Ginger, even if that crazy part of her wished for something more. She couldn't stand to lose anybody else. And if Marcus was really the kind of guy her mother had said he was, the kind who didn't do settling down or family life, then where did that leave them?

Maybe she shouldn't have pushed Ginger to admit that she looked at Marcus like she was starving and he was a big fat steak. But Izzy hadn't been able to help herself. Some hard little part of her had wanted to get under Ginger's skin and find a place that would hurt.

But now…

Now that she knew about Ginger's parents…

Now what?

If Izzy believed in angels, she might think one had just swooped into her life to guide her out of this hell and into a better place.

Was that what Ginger was supposed to be? Did angels come with curly Muppet hair and outfits from Old Navy's two-years-ago collection? Maybe in kids' movies they did.

"Hey," she said, mostly to distract herself from more corny thoughts. "When's Marcus coming back?"

"Anytime now. He went to the hardware store in town to pick up some lumber and supplies to work on the house."

"I thought he was a writer. How does he know how to fix houses?"

"He used to work construction during the summers in college, and before that he was taught carpentry on the commune where he lived for a while with his parents."

"I thought his parents split up."

"They did, but they still lived on the commune

separately, until he was about fourteen, I think. Then he moved to Amsterdam with his dad for his high school years."

"Do you think he'll want to move back there?"

"With you?" Ginger asked. "No, I don't think so. But maybe that's something he should talk to you about, huh?"

"I don't want to go there."

"I think he wants to here stay in the U.S. The threats and all…"

How much would it have sucked if her dad had been killed? And only a few months after her mother died. Well, at least the universe wasn't *that* cruel.

Izzy glanced over at Ginger, who was rolling pizza dough into lopsided round shapes. The universe *had* been that cruel to Ginger.

Losing both parents at the same time? Unexpected tears welled up in Izzy's eyes, and she dropped her knife on the cutting board. No, she wasn't going to start bawling again.

Not now.

Except she was.

Swiping at her eyes, she hurried off toward the bathroom before Ginger could see what was happening. Once she'd locked herself into the cool little room, with its white tile floor and pale blue walls, she was aware that if she let any banshee sounds escape from her throat, they'd probably echo through the whole house, thanks to the acoustics in here.

So she buried her face in the nearest towel and heaved a mighty sob. Grief, her mom had once said, was like getting caught in a whirlpool, and Izzy thought she finally understood what that meant.

It wasn't like going from one place to another. Like, now you're sad, the next day you're a little less sad, and a little less, and then finally one day you're happy.

Instead, you went around and around, feeling the same awful feelings again and again—better, worse, better, worse, worse, worse and worse still. Down, down, she went. Down the toilet.

When the sobs had stopped racking her body, she was sitting on the floor. She could hear Lulu scratching at the door, trying to get in so she could do her tear-licking routine.

A soft knock sounded.

"Izzy?"

It was Ginger.

The last person she wanted to see.

Or…maybe not.

Maybe she wanted to see Ginger, who was living proof that someone could get through having her parents die before she grew up, right when they were supposed to be taking care of her. Ginger looked like she was okay, didn't she?

Izzy tried to shut her brain off to the bad feelings. She stared at the tiles on the floor, visually tracing the lines of white space between them as they made a zigzag pattern across the floor to the door.

"Izzy?" Ginger knocked again softly. "Can I come in?"

At least she knew not to ask stupid questions like, "Are you okay?"

The answer was always no, no, no, of course she was not okay. But Ginger would know that, because she'd been through it.

Maybe Marcus had been pretty smart, after all, bringing Izzy to Ginger's house. Maybe he was trying to take care of her…or pawn her off on someone who knew what to do with her…

She crawled across the bathroom floor and unlocked the door, then pulled it open before sitting back down on the towel. Lulu came barging in first and hopped on her lap, licking anything she could get her tongue on.

Ginger came in and sat down next to her, but she didn't say anything. She just sat there, silent, and Izzy felt some little frozen place in her chest crack open and start to thaw.

MARCUS PARKED IN GINGER'S driveway, his rented truck loaded down with lumber. He loved the way his body felt after a day of physical labor. It reminded him of what a sedentary life writing could be. He usually balanced it by going on long runs, grueling day-long hikes, riding his mountain bike over tough terrain, but all the leisure activity in the world couldn't equal a day of construction work.

He was exhausted, and he loved it, and he hadn't even gotten started on the real work of repairing the house yet.

He climbed out of the truck and crossed the gravel driveway, admiring the simple, classic lines of the house as he approached. No wonder Ginger had fallen for the place in spite of its many obvious flaws. He was happy to be helping her out in this way, giving her a more solid home in exchange for the immeasurable help she was providing him and Izzy.

He entered the house and went to the kitchen, where he was surprised to see the ingredients for making pizzas scattered about, yet no one was around.

"Hello?" he called.

Heading down the hallway, he glanced in each

empty room until he found Ginger and Izzy sitting on the bathroom floor. His stomach tensed at the sudden notion that something was terribly wrong. Izzy's face, red and puffy… She was crying.

They both stared up at him, blinking in surprise at his arrival.

"Is everyone okay?" he asked, knowing it wasn't.

"We're fine," Ginger said quickly. "Just, you know, working through things."

Izzy stiffened visibly, pulling her knees to her chest and crossing her arms over them as she stared at the floor. Marcus wished for the hundredth time that he had even the slightest clue how to help her, what to say, what to do.

So much for the sensitive male he'd always thought he was. All it took was a thirteen-year-old girl to unravel his self-image.

"Did something happen?" he probed, grasping in vain for the right thing to say.

Ginger shrugged. Izzy started shaking her head, but then her shoulders began to shudder and a mournful wail escaped her.

"Ginger's parents," she managed to gasp between sobs, "died…in a car wreck." Then she buried her face in the towel and collapsed in a despair so wretched it shook her entire body.

Marcus gaped at the scene, frozen in terror.

Okay, Ginger's parents had died, what—twenty-something years ago? Hadn't she made that clear to Izzy?

He stared at Ginger, hoping she could make sense of things for him.

She turned from him without missing a beat and directed her attention to comforting Izzy. "It's okay," she murmured as she smoothed the girl's hair back from her face. "Just let it out. Let it out."

The sobs got louder, more mournful, as Izzy lay on the floor shuddering and shaking.

Some part of Marcus split open, baring him to an unwelcome pain. He had felt affection for Izzy before, even the slightest bit of connection, a sense that she was his flesh and blood. But this…this was the first moment when he knew he loved her in a deep-down way that he'd never loved anyone before. And he couldn't bear to see her suffer.

The scent of the lavender bouquet on the bathroom counter teased his senses, and he realized he should be doing something besides standing there like an idiot. The bathroom was too small for him to wedge himself inside and get closer to his daughter. Besides, Ginger was doing a fine job of comforting her.

He opted to kneel down next to Ginger so at least he wasn't towering over them. He watched as her soothing hands and murmurs slowly calmed Izzy down from hysteria to quiet sniffles, and he wondered at the big, intense feelings that had been bottled up in such a slight body. How had she contained all that grief? And how much more was there for her to let out?

Marcus couldn't imagine.

He turned his focus onto Ginger for a moment. Her long hair was swept back into a messy knot, her strong but feminine back only half covered by a halter top. At that moment she was the most beautiful woman he'd ever laid eyes upon. And he was sure it wasn't just intense gratitude coloring his vision.

She turned to him, and he was struck all over again at how beautiful she was. Dear God. How had he never noticed this in college?

"Could you bring her a glass of water and maybe a cool washcloth?"

Marcus got up and retrieved a cloth from the basket on the counter, wet it with cold water and handed it to Ginger. Then he disappeared into the kitchen to get Izzy a drink.

By the time he returned, Ginger was walking Izzy to her bedroom. She took the glass from him and continued on, so he followed behind them, feeling awkward and unnecessary.

"She wants to lie down by herself for a bit," she said to him when they reached the door.

Lulu, who'd been in the bathroom next to Izzy, was now following at her heels down the hallway, and Izzy bent to scoop her up. She carried the dog to the bed and lay down next to her, the crying jag gone but the afternoon still evident on her blotchy face and in her slumped shoulders.

She'd lost something bigger than Marcus could even conceive. She'd lost the one person in her life who'd taken care of her, and he couldn't begin to imagine how he would fill the hole Lisette's death had left.

He couldn't, but maybe Ginger could....

Whoa.

The moment the thought formed in his head, shame washed over him. She'd been a better friend to him than anyone else ever had, and he couldn't ruin that with...with whatever these weird feelings were.

Ginger set the glass of water on the nightstand and placed the washcloth over Izzy's eyes. "This will help with the puffiness. I'll come back in a bit to check on you, but just give us a yell if you need anything, okay?"

The way she took care of Izzy…it must have felt incredibly soothing to the girl. Marcus himself had longed for someone to care for him when he lay in the hospital after the shooting. Occasionally, a nurse would come on duty who had such warmth he felt truly comforted, but for most of them, it was just a job, of course. And he had no one but himself to blame for the fact that the only person who'd attended his bedside was a publicist he barely knew.

As Ginger left the room, he gave her a questioning look. Should he go in? Do something?

She took him by the arm and led him out, then closed the door partway.

Once they were in the kitchen, she turned up the African music playing on her iPod speakers, and leaned in close.

"Let's just give her a little space, and then you can go in if you want to, in a while. But I think she probably just needs quiet right now."

"What set her off?"

"I talked to her about how I'd lost my parents as a kid. I think it brought up a lot of feelings that are just too painful for her."

Ginger began spreading tomato sauce on the pizza crusts.

"What can I do to help?"

"Shred cheese?" She nodded at a hunk of mozzarella and a shredder sitting on the counter.

Marcus got to work, but he kept his attention focused more on Ginger than the task at hand. "You never talked about your parents' death in college."

"No, I didn't."

"Just that one time."

She let out a short laugh, but it sounded hollow.

"The whiskey shots."

"Truth or dare."

"God, I can't believe we did that," she said, shaking her head, a half smile playing on her lips.

"Truth—what's the worst thing that's ever happened to you?" That was what he'd asked her, expecting to hear the kind of answer most people gave. "When my grandmother died," or "When I couldn't swim and my dad threw me in the lake." Not "Being woken up by the babysitter…the police at the front door…both parents killed…drunk driver…"

The image of that scene was forever burned in Marcus's memory even though he hadn't witnessed it. He could imagine Ginger as a girl, groggy from sleep, stunned out of innocence forever.

Or he could almost imagine. Because he'd never gotten close enough to anyone to experience such loss. Even his father's death didn't measure up, because they'd always had a turbulent relationship, and his dad had been so depressed for so many years that he'd already been partly dead to Marcus when it finally happened.

How pathetic that the first huge loss he'd felt was when he'd almost lost his *own* life last month. How very self-centered.

"I didn't talk to people about it, period. I just couldn't. Not back then."

"You avoided me for a week after you told me," he reminded her. He hadn't had a clue what to do back them.

"You never asked me about it again, though. I was relieved."

"I guess I got the hint that it wasn't a welcome subject."

And, of course, it had felt way too intimate, too close for comfort, all that revealing the deepest secrets of their hearts.

"You were the only person at school who knew."

"And now?"

"Now I can talk about it. I tell people if they ask. I don't tell them my parents are living in Australia or anything like that."

Marcus remembered that had been her old stand-by line to keep from having to answer painful questions about her parents.

"What do you think changed to make it easier for you?"

"Years of intensive therapy."

"Oh, yeah, that helps." He'd had a little therapy himself over the years.

"I was so confused after my last boyfriend and I split up, I had to try to understand what went wrong. It felt like the same things were always going wrong with me and men."

She had finished with the tomato sauce and was sautéing chopped vegetables in a skillet as she talked. Marcus had a pile of cheese that looked like enough to cover two pizzas, so he stopped and leaned against the counter to watch her cook.

"I still find it hard to believe you have any trouble with men."

She sighed. "I'm done trying to find Mr. Right. I think I want a kid more than I want a partner, you know?"

"I'm here to tell you, it's not all it's cracked up to be," he said, half joking and half serious.

"Give it a few months. You'll adjust, I bet."

"Have you thought about going the sperm donor route?"

"Yes, but I still wish…I don't know. I guess I have all these ideals when it comes to having a child, adopting a child, whatever. Some part of me isn't ready to just give in and head down to the sperm bank."

"Good," Marcus blurted.

What on earth was he doing?

She said nothing.

"Maybe you'll find another partner," he suggested. "That would make it easier."

Where the hell was he going with this?

He was trying to picture himself in that role. That's what he was doing.

She still said nothing in response.

"So what did you figure out in therapy?"

She looked up from the skillet and met his gaze for a moment, then turned away again. "I figured out that I avoid intimacy to keep from having to experience another big loss in my life."

"Sounds reasonable."

"And I figured out that I hold every guy up to an impossible standard."

"What standard is that?"

"The standard of my idealized version of the perfect man—the perfect love."

Marcus's chest went tight. He frowned, trying to make sense of her words. "What do you mean?"

She half sighed, half laughed, shaking her head. Then she stopped and looked at him. "You never had a clue. You really didn't have a clue, did you?"

He was genuinely lost here. "About what?"

"The fact that I was in love with you all through college."

CHAPTER ELEVEN

THE TIGHTNESS IN Marcus's chest moved up to his throat, and he sputtered, unable to speak.

"What?" he finally managed to croak.

Ginger almost looked bemused. "I was secretly pining after you all that time. I never had the guts to tell you how I felt, because I knew you didn't feel the same."

"Ginger, I…I never knew."

His thoughts became a senseless swirl. Did this mean they might have a chance at— At what? What did he want? He panicked at every idea that formed in his head. Ginger had loved him back then? What about now? What did she feel now?

And what about their priceless friendship?

Looking self-conscious, she turned off the burner on the stove and drained the excess water from the pan. The onions, peppers and mushrooms were nicely browned, beginning to caramelize. She set the pan aside on the stove and took a deep breath.

"I finally figured out that I had fallen for you partly because you were so inaccessible to me. I knew you wouldn't return my feelings, and I knew I could keep you close but not too close. And then for years after, I used those feelings as a barrier to prevent me from getting close to anyone else."

"Wow," he whispered. How had he missed all of this back at school?

"No one else could measure up to a fantasy love that didn't really exist. I mean, I could make you as perfect a lover as I wanted, since you weren't around to upset my fantasies with reality."

"I wish I'd known. I'm sorry I was so…dense."

But was he? a little voice nagged in the back of his mind.

Was he sorry, or relieved? He would never have stuck around as a friend if he'd known how she felt. He'd have run, just as he did from every other woman who'd ever loved him.

"It's better that you didn't know, don't you think?" she said, a wry smile playing on her lips.

What did he say to that?

"Anyway," she continued. "I'm only telling you all this to get it out in the open. I'm in a much better place now, and I value our friendship far too much to mess it up with any weirdness."

"I, uh, I appreciate your telling me all this."

But the feeling growing inside him…he didn't know what it was. It wasn't good, though. Not good at all.

"When I heard you'd been shot, I knew I needed to see you again and reestablish our friendship. But I also had the selfish need to set things right between us so that I could move on with my life and maybe eventually have a healthy, romantic relationship with someone."

"You mean without having to compare them to me?"

"To my idealized version of you, right."

He forced a smile. "Happy to oblige. I can behave like a bigger jerk if that helps."

"No, no, your normal level of jerklike behavior will suffice," she said, not a hint of joking in her tone.

Then she looked up and caught his hurt expression.

"Kidding! I'm kidding," she said, laughing. "I swear."

He laughed along with her, but he felt as if she'd just smacked him in the head with that skillet she was holding.

If he valued their friendship so damn much, why

had he kissed her on his first night in Promise? And why did it feel like a loss to hear she was ready to move on and be nothing but friends?

GINGER WATCHED THROUGH the door for a moment as Marcus sat on the edge of Izzy's bed and talked to her. She didn't want to intrude on them, though, so she slipped quietly down the hallway and into the kitchen.

A half-empty bottle of merlot sat on the kitchen table. She grabbed it, along with her empty wineglass, and went out on the back deck.

The sun was setting, and it was almost dark. The air had taken on the first hint of an early evening chill, but the day had been hot, and was still warm enough for her to sit for a while without needing a jacket. Crickets chirped in the growing darkness, lulling Ginger into a meditative state.

She wanted to escape her thoughts. She didn't want to analyze her conversation with Marcus, what he must be thinking of her now. He must have been freaked out by her admission. She hadn't planned to tell him like that, but it had just come out. Perhaps she'd been keyed up after her talk with Izzy and the girl's subsequent meltdown.

Or perhaps inspired.

Unlike Ginger, Izzy was busy experiencing her

feelings. She was immersed in grief. She walked around with it in her heart every moment of every day, and that had to be healthier than the way Ginger had run from her own grief as a child. Not that she'd had any other option. Like all children, she'd simply been doing what she had to do at the time to survive.

But she didn't want Izzy to go through what she'd gone through as an adult, discovering her unexpressed grief so late in life, a wound that had never been allowed to heal.

Ginger sat in one of the two Adirondack chairs on the deck and propped her feet on the matching ottoman. She poured herself another glass of wine—it would make her third for the night, and she knew she needed to stop there. Any more and she'd risk doing or saying something stupid. Although she'd pretty much dealt with her previous feelings for Marcus, they were still a habit she knew she could fall back into easily if she wasn't careful.

Especially after the kiss…

Footsteps approached from the living room, and she heard the French doors open and close. "Looks like you found the best seat in the house."

"There's another one waiting right here for you," she said, gesturing to the empty chair next to hers.

He'd brought out his wineglass, too, and he sat down and filled it, then lifted it in a toast.

"To you," he said, his slight smile inscrutable.

She wanted to know his thoughts and at the same time didn't want to know them. What did he think of her now?

"To you and Izzy," she said, clinking her glass to his before taking a drink.

"Dinner was great," he said, sounding just the slightest bit awkward.

They'd made it through the meal without much tension. Izzy had provided a welcome distraction. She'd emerged from her bedroom, claiming to be ravenous, once the smell of cooking pizza filled the house.

And true to her word, she'd eaten enthusiastically and appeared to have totally recovered from her meltdown. They'd talked pleasantly, and Ginger had found herself marveling at the ease with which the three of them interacted in spite of the day's drama…or perhaps because of it.

It said a lot for Izzy that she could move past her negative feelings. The day before, she'd been a grumpy, sullen teenager. Now it was as if the dark skies had cleared to reveal bright blue sky.

Maybe it wouldn't last, but it was refreshing to

see a glimpse of the happy girl she must have been before her mother's death.

"Can you believe that?" Marcus said out of the blue.

"Believe what?"

He leaned in and whispered, "Her transformation."

"I'm as amazed as you are."

"It's all thanks to you."

She ignored the compliment. "I think she's starting to relax with both of us."

"Just now, in the bedroom, she was asking if we could stay here past the summer."

Ginger caught his guarded expression. "What did you tell her?"

"I told her I didn't know what would come next, but that we'd figure it out soon."

"You're welcome to stay here with me as long as you want," she said, knowing he was too polite to stay longer than the summer.

"When I left Amsterdam, I knew it was for good. I mean, I knew I was coming back here for Izzy, but I had no idea where we'd be living."

"You didn't give any thought to where you wanted to live?" That shouldn't surprise her, Ginger thought. Marcus had never been much for long-term planning.

"I guess I considered San Francisco, or maybe Santa Cruz since that's where Izzy spent a lot of her life before her mom got sick, but... I don't know. Other times I thought maybe we'd both need a fresh start someplace new, maybe Seattle or San Diego."

"Is your mom still in Seattle?"

He nodded.

"It might be nice to have her help."

"I don't know. She's not really a kid person. Even adult kids apparently, since she hasn't made any effort to see me in years."

"What about Nina? Do you think she has any feelings about custody?"

"Izzy's old enough to choose who she gets to live with, and Nina's fine with that."

"So she's choosing you?"

He shrugged. "She seems to be for now. Who knows what she'll think once she's in the throes of adolescence."

"I hate to break it to you, but I think you're already there."

Ginger sipped her wine, glancing over at him to sneak a quick peek at his profile. But he turned to look at her and their gazes locked.

"I don't know if I can do it," he said, his voice unexpectedly solemn.

"Do what?"

"Raise a teenage girl—alone or even with help. Moments like this afternoon make me realize that it's going to be hard. And it's not like I'm equipped for the job."

"I don't think you have a choice, Marcus," she said carefully, horrified at the notion that he would even contemplate abandoning Izzy after all she'd lost.

"I hate to admit this, but I wonder every day if she'd be better off with Nina. That's who Lisette chose to be her guardian, after all. She didn't choose me."

Fury unexpectedly filled Ginger, and she had to fight to keep her voice even. "That's a cop-out and you know it. She never even gave you the option of being involved in Izzy's life."

"For good reason," Marcus said, almost to himself.

Ginger's hand began to shake, and she slammed her wineglass on the side table too hard, causing it to shatter. She stared at the broken glass and spilled wine as if they made no sense.

"Hey!" Marcus leaned back from the table.

"Don't do that, Marcus." She could barely get the words out, she was so angry. "Don't. Do. It."

"What?"

"Don't run away again," Ginger said through a clenched jaw. "Don't do that to her,"

Shocked by the fury in her voice, he seemed to be struggling not to run away at that very moment. It was what he did when the going got tough, and she saw now why she could never, ever allow her fragile heart to love him as more than a friend.

"I'm not running away," he said, sounding too defensive. "I'm just…just trying to work out what makes sense for everyone involved. And you tell me—what makes more sense? A girl being raised by a strange guy who has no experience with kids, no home, no established connections in this country, or a girl being raised by someone she's known all her life, who loves her and has a home for her and who was chosen by her mother to take care of her?"

The sound of a slamming door caused them both to jump and turn in the direction of the house. Izzy was standing on the other side of the French doors, staring at Marcus as if he were pure evil.

"Izzy," Ginger cried, as she jumped up from her chair and went for the door.

The girl turned and ran through the house, with both Marcus and Ginger chasing after her.

At the front door, she scrambled to unlock it.

"Leave me alone!" she cried as they came up behind her. "Leave me the hell alone! You're a liar and a fake! You're just keeping me here until you can figure out a good excuse to dump me off with Nina again! I hate you!"

Ginger didn't think it would be safe to let her go out into the night, not now, not in this state.

"Izzy, that's not true—you need to calm down," Marcus pleaded, trying to block the door.

Before he could do it, though, Izzy had the door open and was tearing across the front lawn toward the woods. Lulu, upset by the commotion, was standing on the porch barking after her, less brave than her owner when it came to dark forests at night.

"I'll go after her," Ginger said to Marcus. "She's not angry at me."

"But…" He stared at the woods, where Izzy had disappeared.

"Just wait here in case she comes back," Ginger said firmly, then took off after the girl.

She ran as fast as she could, taking care not to trip on any roots, and wishing the whole way that she'd brought a flashlight. "Izzy?" she called. "It's me. Please stop."

That was the problem with troubled girls. They ran. They didn't stick around where they thought they weren't wanted. They ran away.

Ginger's passed a circle of redwoods, and to her surprise found Izzy standing just to the side of the path, staring up at the moon peeking through the trees.

Ginger stopped, breathing hard. "Thank God. Thank you for stopping."

"I heard what he said." Izzy's voice was quiet. "The door was standing partway open, and I could hear. I was just coming out to get another glass of water when I heard my name. I wasn't trying to listen in."

"It's okay. We probably shouldn't have even had that conversation without you there."

"He's going to leave me with Nina, isn't he?" she said, her voice thick with grief.

Ginger swallowed, tried to think of an honest answer that wouldn't condemn Marcus, but she couldn't. She was disgusted with him at the moment.

"He might," she finally said. "I don't know."

"My mom was right about him. He's too selfish to be a father."

Ginger studied Izzy's profile. She could see so much of Marcus in it. She bristled at the idea of Lisette saying such a thing about him, even if it might be true.

She didn't want it to be true, and neither did Izzy. Ginger wanted to believe something big had changed Marcus, that the death threats and the shooting had jarred him out of his easy life and made him wake up to the possibilities he was missing out on. Wasn't that what his return to the States was all about?

Or was it about fear?

Was it about Marcus running away again?

Izzy turned toward her abruptly. "Could I stay here in Promise and live with you?"

Ginger blinked, stunned. "You want to live with *me?*"

"You're the only person I know who understands what it feels like to have your parents die."

"Marcus's father died, you know," she said gently, trying not to sound as shocked as she felt.

"It's not the same. He was already grown up when that happened."

"You're right. It's not quite the same." She reached out on impulse and ran her hand down Izzy's long curtain of hair, smoothing it from her crown to the middle of her back.

"So can I?"

There really wasn't any reason for her to say no. She was already starting to love this girl, and it terrified her. She didn't want to think of how it would feel to have her leave.

"I would be happy to have you stay with me for as long as you want, but it's not my decision."

"It's my decision," Izzy said, "and this is where I want to be."

"What about your school in San Francisco? Won't you miss your friends?"

Izzy shook her head. "I wasn't there long enough to start school. I didn't have any friends in the city. While my mom was being treated at Stanford and we were staying with Nina, I was doing independent study. That's what my mom wanted, so she could spend more time with me."

"How about Santa Cruz? Do you miss being there?"

Another head shake. "I don't want to go back. It would be too sad to be there without my mom."

Up above, an owl hooted from a branch. They both looked up and saw the bird in a nearby bay tree, illuminated by moonlight, staring down at them with its strange eyes.

"Wow," Izzy whispered. "I've never seen an owl before."

As they watched, the bird took off, soaring on broad wings away from them into the night. With its departure, Ginger noticed that the rise and fall of the crickets' song seemed to surround them in stereo sound.

Izzy was staring at her intently in the dark now.

"I don't care where my dad goes. I'm staying here. This is the first place I've been that feels like home."

"I'm glad you like it here," Ginger said gently. "When I first came here, I was really sad, too. I think living here helped heal me."

"What were you sad about?"

"I had broken up with my boyfriend."

"How come?"

Ginger already knew that Izzy deserved her honesty. "He asked me to marry him, and I didn't want to."

"Because you want to be with my dad?"

"No, not exactly. I was afraid. Just like Marcus is now."

"What were you afraid of?"

"Getting too close. Losing my parents made me want to keep everyone away, so my heart couldn't get so hurt again."

"But you wanted to adopt a little girl, right? Why weren't you afraid of that?"

Ginger shrugged. "I don't know. I think I saw it as a chance to heal—to love a child the way I'd wanted to be loved after my parents were gone, you know?"

Izzy said nothing for a moment, but continued to stare at her. "That's why I want to stay with you, see? You could adopt me instead of some girl from China."

Tears sprang to Ginger's eyes. Of course. That was the way a child would view the matter, and Izzy was straddling the line between child and teenager, still able to see things through the lens of innocence.

Ginger couldn't bear to point out all the practical reasons why Izzy's idea might not be possible. Marcus. Nina. Reality. Not right now. Izzy had had enough disappointments for one night.

Instead, she wrapped her arm around Izzy's shoulders and pulled her close, giving her a squeeze. "We should go back to the house. Marcus will be worried."

"I don't want to talk to him tonight," Izzy said when they started walking.

"That's okay. Soon, though, maybe tomorrow, you two need to talk. I can't keep playing the go-between, because the point of this summer is for you to get to know your dad, right?"

"I already know everything I need to know about him."

The cynical adult comment, coming right after Izzy sounding so innocent, nearly caused Ginger to laugh in shock. She wished she had known the girl before tragedy had struck. She imagined Izzy being a confident, sassy thing who knew how to get what she wanted. She'd probably been one of the popular girls at school, which was a world apart from Ginger's own awkward childhood.

But her mother's death had changed Izzy profoundly, Ginger was sure. She herself had gone from being a bookish but confident girl, secure in her happy family, to a sullen child, never quite in step with her peers, never able to fully join in their carefree concerns. And being raised by her grandmother, a sweet little worrywart who dressed her badly and fed her too much, didn't help matters. Ginger ate to soothe herself, and she'd gained weight.

She hoped she could steer Izzy away from the lonely kind of life she'd had, but she also hoped Marcus would find it in himself to give the girl what she needed, too.

"You know," Ginger said as they reached the edge of the woods, "your dad might surprise you. Don't make up your mind about him yet, okay? People never know what they're capable of until a crisis strikes."

"What do you mean?"

"Well, Marcus getting shot, and then learning about you—this is his first chance to prove himself."

Izzy said nothing, and Ginger didn't want to make any hollow promises about what she was sure Marcus would do. She wasn't sure. She had no idea if he'd ever be anything more than the man he'd always been.

So far, he hadn't impressed her.

Marcus was waiting on the porch when they reached the house. He said nothing as they opened the front door to go inside, but he gave Ginger a questioning look. She motioned for him to come in. They followed Izzy to her bedroom, Lulu scampering at their feet. Izzy bent to pick up the dog, avoiding her father's gaze, and Ginger seized the moment to mime that Izzy was going to go to bed and that they should say good-night and leave her alone.

But there she was, playing the gatekeeper again. She needed to get herself out from between Marcus and Izzy. Otherwise, they might never truly connect.

"Good night, Izzy," she said from the doorway as the girl placed the dog on her bed and slipped off her shoes.

"Night," she replied, without looking up.

Ginger started to close the door, but Marcus stopped her. "I need to talk to Izzy," he said, and she resisted intervening.

She simply forced herself to nod and walk away. Izzy was his daughter, after all. Sooner or later he was going to have to learn how to deal with her.

"I don't want to talk to *you*," Izzy said, her voice

rising to a near yell. "Ginger, I told you I don't want to talk to him!"

Ginger sighed and forced herself to go to the kitchen, out of their way.

This wasn't her battle. She had to keep reminding herself of that.

CHAPTER TWELVE

"GO AWAY."

Marcus stepped into the bedroom and closed the door. He probably should have just done as she'd asked, but at least now he had her where he could talk to her, and unless she knocked him down or climbed out the window, she didn't have any means of escape.

"I'm sorry for what you overheard earlier," he said.

She glared at him, then flopped down on the bed and rolled over so that her back was to him.

"Izzy, I only said what I said because I'm afraid I don't know enough about what you need to be a good parent to you."

Silence answered him. Lulu let out a soft whimper, then nestled in beside Izzy.

He had a feeling he was saying all the wrong things, but he was pretty sure there weren't any right things to say, either.

"I want you to help me in the morning," he blurted, recalling that he'd learned carpentry at Izzy's age.

Of course, she looked about as much like a girl who wanted to learn carpentry as he looked like a guy who wanted to wear a pink boa. But still. He had to try something. And he didn't know what else to do.

She gave no reply.

"I want you to do your part to repay Ginger for her generosity in letting us stay here, so you can start working as my assistant first thing in the morning. We've got windows to repair."

He took note of her expensive-looking designer jeans and flimsy halter top. "Oh, and make sure you wear something you can get dirty in."

Finally Marcus started to open the door, but then he paused. He was doing this all wrong, he knew. She didn't want some guy standing in the doorway barking orders at her. She wanted love and understanding. She wanted a shoulder to lean on. That's why Ginger appealed to her and Marcus didn't. He'd been behaving about as warmly as a rock.

He turned and looked at her again, stretched out on the bed, her back to him. He should go to her bedside, he thought. Sit down, put a hand on her shoulder, tell her he loved her.

But even thinking the words made his throat tighten to block them. Saying them aloud…there wouldn't be any taking them back. They'd lay down a world of expectations before him.

He willed himself to go to her and say something loving—anything—but he remained frozen in the doorway, unable to choke out even a simple "good night." Instead he turned and walked out the door, closing it quietly behind him.

He looked around the house for Ginger and found her bedroom door standing ajar, soft lamplight pouring out.

"Hello?" he called quietly. "Can I come in?"

"Yes."

He went into the room and found her standing at the window, looking out into the darkness as she unbraided her hair. She turned to face him. "How did it go?"

He shrugged. "I talked. She gave me the silent treatment."

"I guess that's better than her screaming and throwing things at you." She flashed him a faint smile, but something about her demeanor suggested she was still angry over what he'd said on the deck.

He hated the thought of her being disappointed in him. And as she undid the last part of her braid and her hair fell about her shoulders, he felt as if something important was unraveling before him, something ephemeral and impossible to name. A weight settled on his chest.

"I told her she has to start helping me tomorrow with repairing the house. I thought maybe I could teach her some carpentry."

Ginger laughed unexpectedly.

"What?"

"I…I think that's a great idea. It's just…those fingernails she spends so much time keeping perfectly painted and filed are going to get destroyed."

"That's probably a good thing."

She laughed again, and Marcus breathed a sigh of relief that the tension from a moment before was dissipating.

"You know," he ventured, feeling braver now. "About what you told me earlier, about how you feel, or used to feel about me?"

She nodded, her gaze searching his. "Yeah?"

"I'm flattered."

He'd planned to say more, but the words escaped him. So he crossed the room to where she stood and pretended he was interested in the full moon outside.

"Beautiful tonight, isn't it?" she murmured.

He turned to face her. "You're beautiful, yes."

"Marcus…"

All the latent desire that he'd been working so hard to ignore since their arrival, and then that delicious kiss, came rushing up inside him. He reached out and traced his finger along the delicate line of her collarbone. It was an oddly intimate gesture, probably the most intimate way he'd ever touched her, and he could see gooseflesh popping up on her skin.

His gaze lingered on her chest, on the curves of her breasts that rose slightly above the stretchy fabric of her white top. He could see that she wasn't wearing a bra, and the outlines of her nipples became obvious as her body responded to his touch.

She still wanted him. The evidence was written all over her. And she wasn't pushing his hand away, wasn't backing up. Her lips were parted slightly, and her breathing had quickened.

Of course he knew the signs of a woman's desire, but he didn't know how to navigate this new territory they were traveling, the space between friends and lovers.

A nagging fear tugged at him. He was taking advantage of her. He knew her weakness now, and he was using it against her. For good reason, perhaps. He wanted the best for Izzy, didn't he? Would he have any chance at all of raising her without Ginger's help?

Not likely.

These were the things he told himself while his fingertips explored the soft flesh of her neck, the silken curls of her hair, the firm curve of her shoulder, the long line of her arm.

"What are you doing?" she whispered.

"What do you want me to do?"

The rise and fall of her breasts as she breathed became too much to merely witness. He needed to feel her against him. And whatever she might have said remained unexpressed as he pulled her to him and kissed her.

But this time…

This time he had no intention of stopping unless she told him to. This time, he felt a rush of need so strong he would not be satisfied until he had her against him, without the barrier of clothing between them.

"Marcus," she said breathlessly.

"Do you want this?" He shouldn't have asked, but he saw the signs.

He knew what she wanted.

And she melted into him. "The door," she said. "We should close the door."

Right. He led her to the edge of the bed, then went to do as she'd asked.

A moment later he was back, undressing her, exploring her with his hands and mouth, and before he knew it, they were both naked on the bed, a frenzy of desire propelling them forward without thoughts or words, only instinct.

Here a kiss, there a caress, and there a longing ache that needed satisfaction.

GINGER AWOKE WITH a start, her heart pounding at the sound of someone breathing next to her. Disoriented, she took in the fact that her bedside lamp was still on. And Marcus was lying in her bed, asleep.

She sat up and stared at him, catching her breath from the shock. Okay, so they'd slept together. They were adults. They could handle it.

Dear God.

She watched his chest rise with each inhalation, all smooth skin and sculpted muscle, and memories of every sensation from their lovemaking came back to her. She knew how he felt now, how he tasted. She could fill in all the blanks that used to exist in her imagination.

But her daydreams starring Marcus were about far more than sex. She'd fantasized about lying on a blanket with him, staring up at the clouds, the stars. Talking for hours, laughing, reading to each other—doing all the things they'd done in college as friends. Only this time with the added layer of intimacy that would come, she'd imagined, from being lovers.

Did it really work like that?

Or would that added layer of intimacy only ruin friendship, as some part of her had always feared it would? Bringing on jealousy, insecurity, hurt feelings and mistrust…

What had they just done?

And Izzy…

What if she woke up and discovered them here together? What if she'd already gone looking for Marcus and found his bed empty, and him in Ginger's?

That wasn't likely. They still had time to maintain appearances, to keep Izzy from experiencing the confusion Ginger felt right now.

"Marcus," she whispered, nudging his arm.

He stirred, rolling toward her, but didn't awake.

"Hey, wake up," she whispered, a little louder now, nudging a little harder.

He opened his eyes, frowning in confusion. "Hmm?"

"Wake up. We fell asleep."

"What's wrong?" he asked, then yawned.

"What if Izzy finds us here? You should go to your own bedroom."

He rose up on his elbows and looked around, still groggy. "What time is it?"

Ginger glanced at the clock on the nightstand. "One-thirty in the morning."

"I don't normally get up this early," he said with a wry grin.

"What if she goes for water or something?"

"Is there some reason she shouldn't know what's going on with us?"

His green eyes pinned Ginger with his question. He knew her weakness, and he was using it against her.

She wasn't sure if she had the will to resist him now any more than she had a few hours ago.

"Don't you think it will make a complicated situation even more confusing for her?"

He gave the matter some thought. "I don't like the idea of pretending in front of her. She's old enough to know what's really going on."

"Which is what?" Ginger blurted, before realizing she wasn't sure she wanted to know the answer.

"We slept together."

"I don't think it should happen again," she said, opposing feelings still battling inside her.

What *did* she think?

She needed time to sort it all out. Right now, she mostly felt grogginess and confusion…and fear.

"I'm only sorry it didn't happen sooner. I don't think we've made a mistake, Ginger. Didn't this feel as right to you as it did to me?"

"Of course it felt good. I mean…" She paused, blushing. "I mean, I guess my problem is we're both stressed out and confused, and I think we're just using sex as a distraction."

She could tell by his expression that he didn't buy a word of what she was saying. He had his own agenda, and he fully intended to pursue it.

He cocked one eyebrow, but remained silent for a few moments. "I'm sorry you feel that way," he said in a teasing voice that meant he didn't feel sorry at all.

But he rose from the bed and retrieved his clothes from the floor. He pulled on his jeans for the walk from her room to his, then went to her side of the bed and leaned down so that their faces were only inches apart.

"Night, Gin," he whispered, and kissed her gently on the lips.

When he was gone, she collapsed onto her pillow and sighed. Then she reached over and turned off the lamp.

She lay in the darkness as the minutes ticked past, turning into hours, but sleep wouldn't come to her. Instead her mind raced over the events of the night. Marcus confessing his desire to shrug off fatherhood. Her confessing her old feelings to Marcus, Izzy wanting to live with her... And then the grand finale of the night, this badly timed tumble into bed.

After the emotional turmoil of the evening, it wasn't hard to see why they'd sought refuge in each other's arms, but that didn't make what they'd done any less stupid.

She got up from bed, the clock having just flashed 5:02 a.m., and found a tank top and jeans to put on. After showering, dressing and pulling her hair into a ponytail, she slipped on a robe against the early morning chill and went to the kitchen to make coffee. No sense in wasting any more time waiting for sleep that wouldn't come. She might was well use the quiet to get a little work done.

Ten minutes later, coffee in hand, she sat in her office waiting for the computer to boot up. Her supervisor at the college was expecting her to turn in her syllabus for the summer class she'd start teaching soon, so she could work on that, or she could work on something fun.

Fun meant writing fiction. Unlike Marcus, her

own writing had never met with any great commercial success. She'd published in a handful of literary journals, and occasionally had stories picked up by national magazines, but as she'd told Marcus, her first novel had been a flop, judging by sales, in spite of her prestigious graduate education. If she'd been smart, she'd have done what Marcus had—taken off with a backpack for an education like no other. But she'd been safe, practical. She'd wanted a Master of Fine Arts degree, so she could get a teaching job to support her writing habit.

Classes at the community college would be starting in another week, and this would be her first time teaching Introduction to Writing Short Fiction. Since she needed to write the syllabus, and also develop lesson plans and decide on reading materials, she opted to be responsible and do the work she was getting paid for.

Once she'd started on her syllabus, using a template she'd developed for her other classes, she got lost in the work for a while and was surprised to hear hammering coming from the other side of the house.

Was Marcus up and working already?

She glanced at the small clock in the lower right corner of her computer monitor and saw that it was already past seven. Then she heard the sound of two people hammering at once, and she thought of Marcus's request of Izzy the night before.

No way was the teenager up already. Or was she? Ginger's office was located on the far side of the house from the bedrooms and kitchen, and she had turned music on, drowning out the little noises of an old house, which tended to distract her from her thoughts.

Ginger saved her document, then stood up and stretched, looking out the window for signs of life. Her office faced north, giving her a glimpse of the lake through the trees. The sun was just rising, and the forest and lake still had the misty, soft look of early morning.

She shrugged off her housecoat and grabbed a sweatshirt that lay discarded on the back of her office chair. Pulling it over her head, she hurried out to see what was going on.

Outside, she found Marcus instructing Izzy on how to properly use a hammer and nails. They were practicing on a piece of scrap wood.

"Be sure the nail is at least halfway in before you attempt to hit it that hard," he was saying.

A series of haphazardly bent nails littered the board.

"But you just use a nail gun. Why can't I use one?"

Marcus glanced up from their work when he

heard Ginger's footsteps. "Morning," he said, flashing a beautiful smile.

"Good morning. You two sure are up early." She couldn't see Izzy's eyes, but it wasn't hard to read the girl's posture.

Pure hostility—toward Marcus, or the task at hand, or both.

"I wanted to get out here while it's still cool," he said. "It's supposed to be a hot one today."

Ginger could smell the scent of a hot day coming in the air. She wasn't sure how, but it was a particular scent, indescribable but present.

"It's going to be too hot to work today," Izzy said, taking off the safety goggles she'd probably been forced by Marcus to wear.

"And I told you a couple of hours of work while the air's still cool isn't going to hurt us."

Ginger was impressed that he'd managed to get Izzy out here, and she figured she'd better keep at a distance so Izzy wouldn't be tempted to make her take sides again.

"Have you two eaten breakfast yet?"

"No," Izzy said, oozing sulkiness. "He said we'd eat *later*."

"I could bring out some bagels and cream cheese for you to have while you work," Ginger offered.

Izzy shrugged.

"That would be great." Marcus sent her a meaningful smile.

She wasn't ready to exchange significant looks, so she turned and headed for the kitchen.

"Nail guns are dangerous, and you need to learn basic carpentry skills before you move on to convenience tools like a nail gun," she heard Marcus explain as she walked away.

"I'm taking a break," Izzy said. "This is stupid."

Ginger could hear footsteps following her. She paused at the door and turned to find Izzy right behind her.

"I'll help with breakfast," the girl said.

"I think your dad expects your help out there."

Izzy shrugged. "I'm tired. I'll go back out in a few minutes."

Ginger was still impressed that the teen had gotten out of bed to work so early without a fight. She wondered if deep down, and in spite of their conflicts, Izzy craved one-on-one time with Marcus, but was afraid to ask for it. Ginger made a mental note to test her theory next chance she got.

If true, it would be another piece of evidence that Ginger's presence in their lives could be a hindrance rather than a help.

"Why don't you fill these thermoses with orange juice," she said, taking two silver containers out of the kitchen cabinet.

Izzy went about her task while Ginger put bagels in the toaster.

"So what do you think of working as a carpenter so far?" she asked.

Izzy shrugged. "It's boring, and it's ruining my nails."

"I remember taking a wood-shop class in middle school when I was your age and totally loving it."

"Why?"

"I liked working with my hands, and I liked that at the end, I had something useful to show for my work."

"Oh."

"Just think—when you're done, your work will be a permanent part of this house. Every time I look at it, I'll think of you. That's pretty cool, right?"

"I guess."

Izzy was examining a broken fingernail that had been painted purple with little pink daisy accents.

"Maybe you could do that to your toenails instead of your fingernails. Then you wouldn't have to worry so much about your nails getting ruined."

Izzy cast a hostile glance at her but didn't argue the matter. "Did Marcus sleep in your bed last night?"

Ginger's face flushed, and her throat constricted. Did this girl miss nothing?

"Why do you ask?" she said evenly, as she removed the bagels that had just popped up from the toaster.

"I got up and found his bed empty. I was going to ask him if I could live with you after he leaves."

Ginger paused and turned to look at Izzy. "He was in my room for a while, yes."

"So you two are, like, sleeping together?"

"I'm not sure that's any of your business." She tried to use a joking tone, but the words came out sounding snootier than she'd intended.

"Well, whatever. I can figure stuff out. I'm not stupid."

"I know you're smart, Izzy."

"So you got what you wanted, huh? Are you guys going to be boyfriend and girlfriend now?"

Ginger was surprised by the snide tone. She'd been worried about Izzy getting her hopes up that the two of them would get together. Had she been mistaken?

Was Izzy *jealous?*

"No, I don't think so. We spent some time together last night, but we're still just friends, okay?"

She blushed again, suddenly conscious of the fact that she was supposed to be a good role model for this girl. She was supposed to be modeling healthy, loving adult relationships, not playing a part in their own personal soap opera, complete with a game of musical beds.

But put on the spot this way, she didn't have a clue what to say or do. The issues of parenthood had been thrust on her by surprise, she was failing at every turn.

Izzy looked her up and down, flipped her hair over her shoulder and walked back out the door.

CHAPTER THIRTEEN

"SOMETHING'S DIFFERENT about you," Ruby said as she looked Ginger up and down.

"What do you mean?" Ginger stepped into the house, keys jangling in her hand.

They had a standing date for her to drive Ruby to the Thursday night ballroom dance at the Promise community center. Sometimes they had dinner beforehand, but Ruby had a date this week with a fellow who'd invited her to dinner before the dance.

Ruby cocked her head to the side, nearly knocking off the purple feather fascinator she wore.

"Oh, dear," she said, putting a hand up to steady the tiny hat. "Guess I'd better add a few more bobby pins."

She disappeared down the hallway and came back a minute later still fussing with her hat arrangement.

"I know what it is," she said. "You're falling in love."

Ginger blinked at this news. "No I'm not," she said too quickly.

Ruby offered her a sly look. "I'm old, but I'm not stupid, you know."

"Well, you're wrong." She crossed her arms over her chest, glancing at the ancient cuckoo clock on the wall. "Don't you have to meet your date at six? We should get going."

"A lady's always a few minutes late," her neighbor said, one of her oft-recited maxims.

As she got closer, Ginger could smell the cloying scent of flowery cologne that Ruby had applied liberally.

"Well, you look spectacular," she stated, hoping the topic of love would be dropped.

And Ruby did look amazing. She wore a beaded purple dress that swung dramatically about her legs and revealed her still-enviable décolletage. Her date was going to be floored.

But the very thought reminded Ginger of the way her own body had responded to Marcus's touch. Years of therapy and a small army couldn't have stopped her from falling into his arms.

They left the house, Ruby pausing to lock up, and crossed the yard to Ginger's driveway, where her little white Prius sat waiting for them.

Once they were in the car, headed toward town, Ruby said, "So tell me what's happened with your true love."

"I don't know what you're talking about," Ginger lied.

"You've got that delicious hunk of a man over there living with you, the only man you've ever loved, and you show up on my doorstep today glowing like a lightbulb and expect me to believe nothing's happened?"

"I told you I'm not in love with him anymore."

"Of course you are. True love never dies, especially true love that's never been consummated— or *has* it? Hmm?"

Ginger tried to stay annoyed, but she couldn't fight eighty years of wisdom. She laughed. "You're insufferable."

They rounded a bend in the road and passed the sign for Rainbow Farm. She'd been meaning to get out to Soleil's place for another visit, and made a mental note to take Izzy with her. She had a feeling the girl might even want to do a little volunteer work there now that she was used to getting her hands dirty.

"I imagine you finally stopped kidding yourself and took that gorgeous man to bed, didn't you?"

Ruby was relentless.

Ginger pursed her lips, unsure how much to reveal. "Things…progressed last night."

"Ah-ha! I knew it. You have the telltale glow."

"There's no such thing."

"Of course there is. Oh, maybe it's something about your posture or the lightness of your step or the way your face looks more relaxed— I don't know. But I can see it."

Ginger sighed. "It's a disaster, though. I never should have let it happen."

"You listen to your therapist too much. Tell me, does that woman have a happy love life?"

"I don't know. We don't talk about *her.* We talk about me."

"I'll bet you my fortune she doesn't. You can intellectualize your life all you want, but until you stop thinking about it and start living it with your heart, you'll never find out what's possible for you."

"Maybe I should be paying *you* to be my therapist," Ginger teased.

Ruby laughed, clearly liking that idea. "My Teddy died a happy, happy man."

"Have you ever thought about remarrying?" Ginger asked, deftly steering the conversation away from herself again.

"Oh sure, I've had offers. But I married young

and never got to sow my wild oats, so I figure I ought to spend plenty of time doing that before I settle down again—if I ever do."

Ginger smiled. "What do you mean, 'if'?"

"Most of these old geezers my age are looking for a nursemaid. Someone to take care of them and cook their meals."

"I see."

"It's hard to find anyone who can live up to the standard Teddy set for me. He was a rare find. I got lucky, and I don't expect to get that lucky again."

"You never know."

"So how was it?"

"How was what?" Ginger asked as they arrived at the main intersection in town and waited for the red light to change.

Ruby snorted. "The sex. With Marcus."

"Oh. Aren't you being a bit nosy?"

"I'm living vicariously."

"It was…great," she said, keeping herself in check. No sense in gushing about something that she knew for absolute certain was a disaster, no matter how toe-curling and way better than her wildest fantasies it had been.

"For the sake of that poor little girl, I sure hope you two can come to your senses and stick together."

Ginger had no comeback for that. Maybe in a perfect world, if she and Marcus could fall in love and stay together, they could all be a happy family. It wasn't likely to happen until hell froze over, but didn't Izzy deserve something that resembled a more perfect world after all she'd been through?

"How's she doing?"

"Izzy? She's okay, I guess. Not quite as volatile."

"I saw her out there working with her dad. That was a good idea—whoever thought of it."

"Marcus did. Yeah, I think it's giving her something else to focus on, and she's even starting to like it, now that she's getting better at handling the tools."

They pulled into the parking lot of the Trattoria Ginolina, where Ruby was scheduled to meet her latest beau.

"Thank you for the ride, my dear."

"You're welcome. Have fun."

Ruby paused halfway out of the car, the feathers on her fascinator brushing against the roof. "Just think about that girl, is all. Think about what she needs."

"She told me she wants to live with me."

"Of course she does. You two are kindred spirits. You have the same hole in your heart." Ruby reached out and patted Ginger's hand, then climbed the rest of the way out of the car.

"Oh, are we still on for you to drive me to my doctor's appointment tomorrow?"

"Absolutely," Ginger said.

"Bye-bye!" Ruby called as she entered the restaurant.

Ginger waved and drove away, her mind spinning. She knew, of course, how much it would have meant to her to have had an intact family while growing up. The ache was so deep she still felt it. Granny Townsend, loving as she was, couldn't replace what she'd lost.

And Ginger could never replace what Izzy had lost.

But she did know her pain. She knew it well.

And knowing it, she couldn't ever add to it. She knew Ruby was right—she had to do whatever she could to help Izzy grow into a happy, secure person. Everything in her life had been leading her to that very purpose.

OKAY, SO CARPENTRY wasn't quite as stupid as Izzy had thought it would be.

Sometimes it was even fun.

A week after she'd started working with her dad on the house, she was really getting into it. Sometimes she pretended she was one of those people on the reality TV shows, fixing up a house for some person who'd written in to ask the show for help.

She wiped her sweaty hands on the old jeans she'd bought with Ginger yesterday at the secondhand store, and went to the workbench to get her water bottle.

She and Marcus had spent the morning measuring and cutting wood, and now they were about to start demolition on the second window to be repaired—the one in Izzy's room. At least, she'd come to think of it as her own.

She believed Ginger really did want her to stay. She could tell when adults were lying, and Ginger was definitely telling the truth.

But she didn't know yet what Marcus thought about staying in Promise, and she was afraid to ask. Which was weird.

Izzy had never been afraid of asking questions. She'd been kind of famous at her old school for asking teachers questions that no one else would have dared to ask. Like "Mrs. Dupinski, why do you write the same comments on our papers, no matter what we say?" And "Mr. Floyd, do you really think no one knows you're having an affair with the vice principal?"

That second one had gotten her detention for a week.

The late-morning sun was just starting to heat up, and already Izzy's body ached from work. She was hot and tired, and she wore grungy clothes she wouldn't have been caught dead in a week ago. Her hair, pulled back in a ponytail, hadn't been washed yet today, and she wasn't wearing a spot of makeup. Not even concealer, which she used to be terrified of leaving the house without.

Izzy smiled to herself. This was what the country life was doing to her. Turning her into a sweaty, unstylish tomboy.

But the funny thing was, she felt better than she had for as long as she could remember. Maybe the last time she'd felt this good was when she'd been a little kid running around, getting dirty, not caring about anything but having fun.

Marcus came over and took off his work gloves, then grabbed his own thermos. "I'm hungry," he said. "What do you say we take an early lunch break?"

"Sure," Izzy said, shrugging.

She'd been pissed at Marcus for the first few days they'd worked together, but there was something about him that made it hard to stay mad.

He was nice. He wasn't like a lot of adults, who talked to kids like they were just dumb kids. He talked to Izzy like she was an adult. And he was patient when she screwed things up. Which she did pretty often.

And he made her laugh. Like when Lulu kept getting under his feet yesterday. Instead of getting mad at the dog, he'd picked her up and put the work goggles on her, then acted like he was teaching her how to level a window frame. Then for the rest of the day, he kept acting like he was teaching the dog carpentry lessons, when it was really Izzy he was teaching.

They went inside now, and Izzy got all the sandwich ingredients she could find out of the fridge. This had become their lunch routine. They'd put everything on the table and see who could make the most creative sandwich. That was the cool thing about Marcus—he could even turn fixing lunch into a game.

"Where's Ginger?" Izzy asked, wishing she was around to join them.

"She had to take Ruby to a doctor appointment in Santa Rosa. They're supposed to be back this afternoon."

"Oh."

"Didn't she ask if you wanted to go along and go shopping in town with her?"

"Uh-uh."

"She said she was going to, but I complained about her taking my assistant away. I guess she figured you'd want to stay and work." He flashed her a grin that said he knew she'd much rather have gone shopping.

Izzy rolled her eyes.

"Hey, I was wondering," he said as he sat down at the table and started opening a jar of pickles. "Did your mom ever get married or have a serious relationship?"

Izzy watched him closely, wondering how he felt about that. When she was younger, she used to fantasize that her dad would reappear and marry her mom and they'd all live happily ever after.

"She didn't get married, but she had boyfriends."

"Did any of them ever live with you?"

"Yeah, Jay did. For a few years."

"And then they broke up?"

"Then my mom got sick, and he didn't want to stick around to watch her die."

Marcus's face went hard. "That's pretty lousy."

Izzy shrugged. She'd been kind of relieved to see him go. She used to have her mom all to herself before Jay moved in.

"Yeah, I guess so."

"Did you get along with him?"

"I guess. He didn't really pal around with me or tell me what to do."

"He didn't try to be a parent to you."

"No." Izzy busied herself slicing avocado for an avocado, cheese and veggie sandwich.

"Will you make one of those no-meat sandwiches for me, too?"

"With pickles?" she asked, since all his sandwiches contained pickles.

"You decide."

She worked in silence for a minute. Then she said, "Why'd you ask about Jay?"

"I've been wondering if I'm one of a long string of guys who've come along and tried to be your dad."

"But *you* are my dad. You don't have to try, right?"

He shrugged. "It seems more like a right I should have to earn, don't you think?"

"No," she said without looking at him.

Something about this conversation was making her throat get all tight and her eyes burn. She didn't want him auditioning for the role of dad in her life, because that meant he could decide not to show up for the tryouts. He could just vanish if he didn't like the part. Like he'd already hinted he would.

"You think biology trumps performance?" he asked, his tone teasing now.

"I guess."

"How about social studies?"

"What?"

"Sorry, bad joke. I can't be on my game all the time. So what was this Jay guy like?"

"Are you sizing up your competition?"

"Absolutely."

Izzy finished making the first sandwich—whole-wheat sourdough bread piled high with avocado, Monterey Jack cheese, sprouts, lettuce, tomato, pickles and mayonnaise. She put it on a plate and pushed it across the table to Marcus.

"Now that's a work of art."

He picked it up and took a bite, while Izzy started assembling her own sandwich.

"Jay looked pretty different from you. He was small and kind of nervous. But he was a musician. He played jazz guitar, and he went on the road a lot, and my mom kind of didn't like that. They fought about it sometimes."

"Was he nice to you?"

"Yeah, I guess. But I thought he needed to, I dunno. Grow up?"

"Why is that?"

"'Cause he was older than my mom and still trying to be a rock star, you know? He didn't have a real job and didn't want to get married and didn't want to have kids, but just wanted to have fun."

She glanced up and caught Marcus looking kind of weird. As if he didn't like what she was saying, and then, in an instant, she knew why. Because Marcus was kind of like Jay.

Maybe her mom had liked a different type of guy than Izzy had thought—maybe she liked irresponsible guys who couldn't grow up. Marcus didn't want to get married or have kids or get a real job. He just wanted to run off and have fun, far as she could tell.

When she thought of it like that, she wanted to fling all the food off the table and break the dishes.

"How about your mom? Did she want to settle down and get married?"

"I guess. I don't know. She talked like she didn't, but she was always depressed after any of her boyfriends disappeared."

"Do you understand that if I'd known about you, I would have been a part of your life?"

Izzy blinked at this, trying not to tear up.

"You mean you would have married my mom?" she said, once she could speak again.

"I don't know about that. Your mom and I were young and fought a lot when we were together. I'm not sure how happy any of us would have been if we'd stayed together. But I definitely would have wanted to be a father to you."

"From Amsterdam?"

"No, I mean, I guess I would have moved closer—"

"You *guess?*"

He sighed. "I can't say what would have happened, but I'm here now, okay?"

"For the moment."

She placed a piece of bread on top of her sandwich, but she no longer had an appetite. She thought about what her dad had said about leaving Promise, about returning her to Nina and her perfectly stylish house in San Francisco....

"That's not what I meant."

Izzy picked up a stray bean sprout from the table and pretended to be interested in it twirling it between her fingertips. Under the table, Lulu was hovering near her feet, waiting for her to drop something interesting. Sprouts didn't count as interesting to the Chihuahua.

But Izzy was afraid to let Marcus speak to her. She didn't want to make him say something she didn't want to hear.

He bent down and came up with Lulu in one

arm. He placed the dog on the table, amid all their sandwich fixings.

"Shh, don't tell Ginger."

"That's gross. Her feet are dirty."

"Oh, right," he said, and scooped up the dog again, placing her on his lap. "Lulu, don't you know to wash your paws before you come to the table?"

He picked up his napkin and wiped the dog's front paws with it. Then he put her paws on the edge of the table as if she was waiting to eat.

"She doesn't like vegetables much," Izzy said.

"Oh? You haven't trained her to be a vegetarian, too?"

Izzy rolled her eyes. "She's a *carnivore*."

Marcus raised one eyebrow. "Are you sure? She doesn't look like she falls into the same category as a wolf or a lion."

"I think Chihuahuas were bred to hunt, like, rats and mice and stuff."

"Oh. I see. And you're not opposed to that, as a vegetarian?"

He was teasing her again, and she was kind of relieved to have them talking about something not so serious.

"I'm not going to make my dog be a vegetarian, okay? That's dumb."

He tried unsuccessfully to get Lulu to eat a piece of lettuce. But she went for the slice of avocado he offered.

Marcus looked up at Izzy. "I only meant earlier that I wish I'd known you as a kid. I wish I could have watched you grow up to be the kid you are today. I'm sorry I missed all that."

Izzy took a bite of her sandwich, because she didn't know what to say. And she kept her eyes on her plate, because she was afraid if she looked at her dad, she'd start bawling like a baby.

What he'd said… It felt kind of like something she'd been waiting her whole life to hear, and she didn't want to ruin the feeling by saying the wrong thing.

CHAPTER FOURTEEN

GINGER'S FIRST DAY of teaching at Promise Lake Community College was a success. Her students seemed eager and engaged, and her course load was light enough that she could still spend time with Izzy…and Marcus.

Nearly a week had passed since they'd slept together, and so far they'd managed to pretty much pretend nothing had happened. She didn't want to talk about it, and he didn't seem to care one way or the other.

Back at home, she put down her school bag and headed toward the sounds of life coming from the kitchen. Jazz was playing on the iPod speakers, and the scent of something garlicky and delicious filled the air.

"Hey," Marcus said, smiling when he spotted her in the kitchen doorway. "You're home just in time."

She took in the sight of the dining room table, bedecked in candles and set for dinner.

"Wow, what's the special occasion?"

Izzy placed a basket of bread on the table. "He's not telling. It's some big secret."

Marcus, looking ridiculously sexy in Ginger's green gingham apron, smiled. "Oh, just a little good news. I'll tell you when we're all sitting down."

With a pot holder in one hand, he removed a pan of lasagna from the oven.

Ginger inhaled and instantly felt hungry. "Anything I can help with?"

"No, just have a seat. Everything's ready."

Izzy sat down in her usual spot, put her elbows on the table and then, seeming to remember her manners, removed them again.

Marcus brought the lasagna to the table and placed it on a couple of extra pot holders he'd managed to unearth. Ginger had always liked the fact that Marcus knew his way around a kitchen, but this was his first time breaking out the domestic skills here at her house. He'd been so busy with the repair work, she imagined he hadn't had the energy to do more.

She eyed the bottle of champagne Marcus produced and began pouring, and her stomach flip-flopped. *Champagne?*

When he finished, he picked up his glass. "I'd like to make yet another toast, since that seems to be what we do around here." His eyes twinkled, but he offered no further explanation.

Ginger lifted her glass, and Izzy, looking as perplexed as Ginger felt, raised her own flute of apple juice.

"You have to tell us what we're toasting, you know," Ginger said.

"Okay." He paused, clearing his throat. "I got a call from my literary agent today. She said my publisher is offering me a big, big contract to write a memoir of my experience living with the death threats and being shot."

"Marcus, that's great! Congratulations!"

They toasted, and then Ginger thought to ask, "But wait, is this a book you didn't even pitch?"

He shook his head. "Me? Write a memoir? It's not exactly my chosen genre, but for the money they're offering, I think I can work up the enthusiasm to do it."

"Wow."

"It's great timing. I've been starting to wonder what my next project would be."

"You mean working on my house isn't satisfying your creative urges?"

"It does, actually—which scares me," he said with a wry smile.

Izzy was listening to their exchange quietly, and Ginger wondered what the girl was thinking.

Marcus continued. "They also want me to pick up my book tour for *Seven Grains of Sand* here in the U.S. now that I've recovered."

Finally, Izzy spoke up. "What does that mean?"

"It means I'll be traveling for a while, maybe six months."

Ginger stared at him, aghast. Did he understand what this meant for Izzy? He was smiling, clearly oblivious to the fact that his daughter shrank back in her chair at his words.

"But—"

"It's much safer to do a book tour here. I don't think we have to worry about a repeat—"

"What about Izzy?" Ginger blurted before realizing she probably should have asked this question in private.

"I don't know. We'll have to figure that out. You could stay with Nina while I'm gone, right? Or maybe here with Ginger?"

He didn't get it. He was so drunk on his good news, he really didn't get it.

Izzy glared at him, saying nothing. The only

sound in the room was Lulu's toenails clicking on the hardwood floor as she moved around.

Then, as if in slow motion, Izzy raised the hand holding her juice. The glass flew across the room and landed against the wall with a crash. Their second smashed drinking glass in a week. At the impact, time went into fast-forward. Izzy racing from the room. Marcus staring at her, stunned, a reprimand frozen on his lips.

And Ginger understood him perfectly in that instant as she rose and followed Izzy. He was frozen in terror, both literally and figuratively—afraid to assert his authority as a father, because doing so would make him one not just in name but in fact.

Running away on a book tour was by far the easier option.

The cowardly option.

The option he'd always chosen.

Izzy's door slammed just before Ginger reached it, and she heard the click of the lock.

"Izzy, please let me in," she called, but wasn't sure what she'd say if she was allowed in.

Yes, your father is an idiot. Yes, he's an ass. No, he's not really father material at all.

Your mother was right all along to have left him out of the equation.

Ginger pressed her forehead against the cool, grooved wood of the door frame, her hand resting on the knob. "Izzy?" she tried again.

Nothing.

Marcus came down the hallway and stopped beside her. "Open the door, Izzy," he said. "We need to talk."

But even Ginger could hear the uncertainty in his tone, as if he wasn't quite sure he belonged there, telling her to do anything.

First chance he had to return to his glamorous literary life, and he already had one foot out the door?

The writer in Ginger recognized the lure. Didn't every writer at times long to escape the complication of human interactions for the self-centered pursuit of one's own creative vision?

Over the years, Ginger had matured. She'd come to see her writing for what it was—one facet of her life, not more or less important than any other part. And in truth, it was often less important to her than the everyday, unglamorous act of helping a student find his or her own writer's voice.

Marcus tried to grab the doorknob, and she let her hand fall away. Who was she to interfere now? Doing so hadn't helped anything so far.

As he shook the door, she turned and walked

toward the living room. She went out the French doors onto the deck and leaned against the railing. Lulu followed her, so she scooped up the little dog and held her close.

"All this drama," she whispered. "You're the only one here who stays calm."

Marcus stepped outside a moment later.

"She's got to stop with these tantrums," he said, shaking his head as he sat down on an Adirondack chair.

Ginger bit her tongue. What did she know about raising a teenager, anyway?

When she looked at Marcus, her heart split in two. One part had always foolishly loved him, and one part, the wiser part, saw his ugly side and loathed his selfishness.

"So you're just going to *dump* her with someone and go on a book tour?"

She couldn't bite her tongue, after all.

Pure fury was rising up inside her. It was the fury of a mother bear protecting its cub.

He stared at her, shock registering in his eyes. "You think she's better off with me? Look what just happened. We try to have a nice dinner, and a glass gets smashed against the wall. She storms off and locks herself in her room."

"That's called having a teenager. A teenager who just lost her mother, by the way."

He shook his head, his shoulders slumped. "I'm not cut out for this. I thought I could handle her, but I can't, okay?"

Ginger wanted to shake him. She wanted to slap some sense into him. But she couldn't even find words.

He went on. "Besides, I have to earn a living, and the better my current book does, the better my next one will sell."

"Grow up, Marcus."

"What?" He blinked at her, incredulous.

"Grow the hell up! Stop thinking about your own damn ego and think about what's best for your daughter for once!"

Ginger hadn't meant to yell, but the fury had come bursting forth, and there was no stopping it now.

"Ginger—"

"You think the number of books you sell is more important than giving that child a chance to feel safe and secure and loved?"

"Of course not, but you can see that this isn't working. I'm not giving her what she needs."

"What happened to us becoming a big happy family? Wasn't that your idea?"

His expression turned darker. "Does this feel like a happy family to you?"

"I don't want you here anymore," she said. "Izzy can stay, but I think you should leave."

"Okay," he said evenly. "Should I leave tonight?"

"No," Ginger said, tears springing to her eyes. "Wait until tomorrow so we can talk to Izzy when she's calm."

How could she sit there and tell the girl she was about to lose another parent? How could Marcus?

She started to walk inside, but he stood and caught her by the arm. "Ginger, I'm sorry. I thought maybe this could work. I didn't want it to turn into something ugly."

And she understood then why he hadn't pushed the issue of what their lovemaking had meant. After the initial rush of excitement, the messy details of figuring out whether or not they could work as a couple were too much for him. He'd taken the coward's way out.

With that, she shook her arm loose from his grasp, turned and went inside. Lulu still in her arms, she went to her room and closed the door, lay down on the bed and cried.

CHAPTER FIFTEEN

IZZY HAD NEVER hitchhiked before. She'd seen other people thumbing for a ride on the side of the road, and of course her mother had told her to never, ever, ever do it because of bad people and all that. But her mom was gone now, and her dad didn't give a damn, so who was going to stop her?

She walked along the side of the road that led out of Promise toward the highway, making up a story for whoever stopped to pick her up. She would say she was sixteen, not thirteen, and that she'd been on her way to stay with her cousin in Los Angeles when her car broke down.

She carried most of her things in a backpack, and had tucked Lulu into the doggy travel bag with her head peeking out. No one would hurt a girl carrying a tiny dog, right?

She'd also have to tell the person who picked her up that her dad was abusing her and that she was going to stay with relatives who'd keep her safe. That way no one would try to take her back to Promise and hunt down her parents.

This time of morning, with the sun just about to rise, was an odd time for someone to be hitchhiking, but she couldn't have waited around any longer. She hadn't wanted to leave at night, so she'd slept for a while, then crawled out the window at dawn, a few hours before anyone would check to see if she was awake.

The cool morning breeze caused her to shiver, and she tried not to think about how scared she was. That would only cause her to shiver more. No, she wasn't going to be scared. It didn't really matter what happened to her anyway.

No one cared all that much, so why should she?

Once she did get to L.A., she wasn't sure what she'd do, but it seemed like the place to go if you were a runaway teenager. She remembered seeing what had seemed like hundreds of them in Hollywood when she'd visited there a few years ago with her mom. So at least she wouldn't be alone.

But she did worry about money—she had only forty dollars, left over from her last birthday—and food. How would she get any? She'd have to ask the other homeless kids. There were soup kitchens that gave away free food to them right?

What about Lulu? Would they feed dogs at a soup kitchen? It didn't seem likely, but she'd seen homeless people with dogs....

God, she didn't want to be on the street. She didn't want to go back to Nina's, either. Marcus would find her there, and then he'd get to be all smug that she was being well taken care of. Like he'd done the right thing, leaving her with her godmother.

The longer she walked along the side of the road, the more things Izzy could think of to worry about. But she wasn't going back. She wasn't going to give Marcus the satisfaction of leaving her behind. She wasn't going to let another parent abandon her.

She did feel bad about leaving Ginger, but Ginger would be fine. She could still adopt some cute little Chinese kid who wouldn't argue or slam doors, and it would be a lot more fun than having Izzy around.

A car approached, and Izzy raised her thumb, only her fourth chance so far to catch a ride. But the white car just kept going like the rest had; the driver didn't even slow down or give her more than a glance.

Memories of the night before invaded Izzy's thoughts.

It was easy to tell when adults had bad news, because they didn't want to look you in the eyes.

They started acting weird, too, but they figured you were too dumb to know something was up.

Izzy had known something bad was about to go down as soon as Marcus started making dinner, acting like he'd drunk too much coffee. He'd let her help when she offered, but he hadn't wanted to tell her why he was in such a frenzy.

For a short, foolish while, she'd kidded herself into believing maybe he was going to propose to Ginger. Or that he'd already proposed and they just needed to break the news to Izzy that they were getting married.

God, she could be so stupid.

So, so stupid.

But it hadn't taken long for her to realize that whatever was going on, it wasn't good news for her. If it had been, Marcus would have looked her in the eye. And he'd have told her what was happening. He wouldn't have kept her waiting.

Lulu whimpered, and Izzy stopped walking to cover the dog with the little blanket she'd wiggled out of.

From behind her came the sound of another car approaching. Then headlights appeared, rounding the bend in the road. She could see now that it was a truck, not a car. A big semi. As it passed, she stared at the driver and motioned with her thumb.

And something miraculous happened.

The truck slowed, then pulled to the side of the road ahead of her and stopped.

Izzy's heart pounded about a mile a minute. She wanted to puke. God, was she really going to do this? Get in that truck with some stranger?

What other choice did she have?

She jogged to catch up, and as she got closer, the truck's passenger door popped open. She climbed onto the step below the door and peered in at a gray-haired man with a beard and a big belly.

"Can I…um, have a ride?"

"Where you headed?"

"L.A."

"I'm going as far as Bakersfield. You're welcome to ride along."

Bakersfield. Where was that? North? South? Did it matter? She'd figure it out later. For now, this was the only chance she had to get away from Promise.

Izzy climbed into the truck and shut the door.

"Hi, I'm…Josie," she said, giving the name of one of her best friends from childhood. "And this is Lulu." She nodded at the bag. "You mind having a dog in the truck?"

"Don't suppose I do," he said as he pulled out onto the road again.

And that was it. She was on her way. Somewhere.

Away from Marcus.

Away from Ginger.

Away from everything that was never going to be.

"HAVE YOU SEEN IZZY?" Ginger asked.

Marcus was already packed, his suitcase standing next to the door, when Ginger found him putting on his shoes in the living room. Her heart sank for the second time in the past few minutes.

"I thought she was sleeping in," he said.

"Were you going to leave without saying goodbye to her?"

"Of course not. I just didn't want to wake her. I figured I'd hang around until she got up."

Hang around where? Ginger wanted to demand. *In your car with the engine on?* But she bit her tongue.

She was the one who'd asked him to leave, after all.

"She's not in her room. I just looked."

"Where is she then?" he asked.

"I was hoping you'd know. It looks like she left in a hurry."

"What about Lulu?"

"She's gone, too. Maybe Izzy took her for a walk, but Lulu's bag is missing, and I've got a bad feeling…."

"Her bag is missing?" He was a few steps behind Ginger in putting the facts together.

Already her hands were shaking, and she wanted desperately to pick up the phone and call the police—run out the front door and launch a search party. She needed to do something, anything, to make sure Izzy was safe.

"She wouldn't run away, would she?" Marcus sounded confused, as if he couldn't imagine a distraught, angry teenager ever thinking of doing such a thing.

"Why not?" Ginger nearly screeched, her voice rising. "Why would she want to stick around here?"

"She loves it here." He paused, seeming to consider the possibilities. "She said she wanted to stay here with you."

"Maybe she changed her mind."

Marcus expelled a ragged breath and ran a hand through his hair. "Okay, so let's start looking. I'll go down to the lake, where she likes to walk. You check around here?"

Ginger nodded, relieved to have a course of action. "I'll also check with Ruby to see if she's seen or heard anything. And I'll call Nina, too."

Marcus nodded. "If I don't find her by the lake, I'll circle back through the woods and look for her there."

"Bring your cell phone and call me if you find her. I'll do the same." Ginger headed back to Izzy's room to look for clues.

She had a strict policy against nosing around, and even now, under potentially dire circumstances, something in her rebelled against violating the girl's privacy. But necessity propelled her farther into the room, which was flooded with morning light.

The east-facing window stood partway open, but Ginger knew Izzy kept it like that to cool the room at night, since the house had no air-conditioning. The screen was still in place, so if she'd left in the night, she had to have gone through one of the doors.

The bed was unmade, its white sheets and flower-print quilt a tangled mess. That, too, was normal. Izzy didn't make the bed unless asked to do so.

Ginger went to the desk and rummaged around, finding nothing amiss. Then she looked in the closet and noticed that Izzy's jacket wasn't there. Also missing were several outfits, and the girl's purse, which she normally kept on top of the chest of drawers.

Ginger would have to check the laundry to confirm that the clothes were really missing, though, so she went down the hallway to the bathroom and searched the near-empty hamper, then went to the hall closet that housed the washer and dryer. Nothing in either place belonged to Izzy, except for one sweatshirt she'd spilled wood stain on while working with Marcus.

Back in the bathroom, Ginger checked for Izzy's toothbrush, but it was gone, along with the small pink bag of cosmetics she usually kept on the bottom shelf of the medicine cabinet.

Ginger's stomach felt hollowed out. Where would the girl have gone? And how had she intended to get there? As far as Ginger knew, Izzy had no money and no friends who drove.

Oh, God.

What if…

What if she intended to hitchhike?

Or what if she wasn't headed anywhere at all? What if she was suicidal?

The moment the thought formed in her head, Ginger tried to banish it. But she pictured the wide, cold expanse of Promise Lake. Maybe the idea of swimming until she grew tired might seem better than the other options Izzy faced. Ginger pictured the deep, dark sadness she'd seen more than once in Izzy's eyes, and cold fear shot through her.

She wouldn't, would she?

Ginger went to the phone and dialed Ruby. It was

just after nine in the morning, and her neighbor normally rose with the dawn light. If anyone had seen anything fishy, it would be her. She answered on the third ring with a friendly "Hello?" Ginger explained the situation, but Ruby hadn't seen Izzy.

Another phone call confirmed that Nina hadn't heard from Izzy, either. Her worried tone reminded Ginger that it was her fault—hers and Marcus's—that Izzy was missing now. Nina promised to let Ginger know first thing if she heard from Izzy, and she said she'd call around to alert any of Izzy's friends that she might run to for shelter.

After hanging up the phone, Ginger went out onto the front porch to watch for Marcus. He hadn't called, which meant he hadn't found anything. Maybe she'd be better off searching the woods, too….

Or was it time to call the Promise Police Department? Her throat tightened at the thought. God, what if…

No, she had to stop with the what-ifs. They weren't helping. Now was the time to remain calm and clear headed.

Wherever Izzy was, they would find her. Ginger had to believe that.

CHAPTER SIXTEEN

MORE THAN TWENTY-FOUR hours since she'd disappeared, and they still hadn't found Izzy.

Marcus jumped each time the phone rang, which was why he'd had to get out of his hotel room and do something. Almost every call had to do with his agent or his publicist, though. Schedules were being rearranged. People were upset with him. He was supposed to be starting his book tour with a reading in San Francisco tomorrow.

His whole life had turned into a surreal nightmare.

And the hours continued to tick by without any word from Izzy. No news of what had happened to her.

Ginger had been frantic to find Izzy, but she hadn't been willing to let Marcus stay. She'd insisted he had to leave, though she'd already called several times to check in and insist again that he phone her the moment he heard anything.

Marcus stood in front of the color copy machine

at the Promise Quick Copy shop and watched as flyer after flyer spat out.

This was what his stint as a father had been reduced to—making copies of a Missing Person flyer for his daughter.

He'd failed in an even bigger way than he could have imagined, and finally, he understood that this wasn't about him.

This wasn't about him.

It was about Izzy.

Too late he realized that parenting wasn't an interesting experience for him to partake in, to further round out his life and achieve personal growth. It was about raising a child as best he could, strictly for that child's sake, so that she might grow up and have something positive to contribute to the world.

Why couldn't he have understood that from the start? If he had, this might never have happened. Izzy would be safe, and Ginger wouldn't hate him for the selfish bastard he was. And he wouldn't hate himself.

He picked up the stack of five hundred copies, then went to the counter to ask if he could post one in the store window.

He almost couldn't look at the flyers, but

forced himself to read a copy one last time to make sure the phone numbers and contact information were correct.

Izzy's pretty, vaguely petulant face stared back at him. The photo was maybe a year old; it was the one she'd e-mailed to him before they met.

Isabel Grayson, aka Izzy, thirteen years old, missing from Promise Lake, California...

Tears welled up in his eyes, and he wanted to smash something, anything—smash everything into a million little pieces.

He loved that girl. He loved her, and if he got another chance, he'd do anything he could to make her happy.

The woman at the counter stared at the flyer.

"This your girl?" she asked.

He nodded, unable to speak.

"I'll be happy to post it for you, hon. And if you give me a little stack I'll make sure the rest of the businesses around here do the same, okay?"

"Thanks," he managed to croak.

"Such a shame," she said. "Poor thing."

He turned and left with the stack of flyers before he shouted at the woman. His daughter wasn't a shame. She wasn't a poor thing. She wasn't going to end up as a statistic, a face on the side of a milk carton.

He would find her, and she would be safe, and that's all he could allow himself to believe right now.

WHEN GINGER saw Marcus's car pull into her driveway with a thirteen-year-old girl alive and well in the passenger seat, she nearly passed out with relief.

The phone call hadn't been enough to convince her that Izzy was okay. She'd needed to see her in person.

And she still wasn't convinced. She needed to hug Izzy close, look into her eyes and sense with her gut whether there was any hidden damage, anything the girl might be afraid to tell them.

Ginger hurried out the front door and raced down the steps and across the grass. As soon as Izzy, looking tired and bedraggled, opened the door and got out, Ginger swept her into a big hug that went on and on.

"Thank God," she whispered into Izzy's hair. "Thank God you're okay."

Then she pulled back to look her in the eyes. "*Are* you really okay?"

Izzy, her expression self-conscious now, shrugged and stared at the ground. "Yeah, I'm fine. And I'm sorry for running away and worrying you so much."

"Is that what your dad told you to say?"

"I told her she owed you a year's worth of free carpentry work," he said.

Ginger looked up, almost shocked to find him there.

He looked tired, too, more tired than she'd ever seen him. As if he hadn't slept in days.

And if he hadn't, good for him. He deserved some sleepless nights.

Okay, maybe she was being a bit unfair, but she wasn't about to make any more excuses for Marcus.

"I'll be able to...I mean, I could keep helping with the house if you want me to, because we're going to stay in Promise," Izzy said, smiling tentatively.

"You are?" Ginger looked from her to Marcus for confirmation.

We? Did that mean both Izzy and Marcus?

"I canceled the book tour. Told my publisher I have more important things going on in my life right now that need me to stay put."

Ginger blinked. She knew better than to take such an about-face as the final word on the matter. Surely he'd change his mind once the reality of having to live the small-town life as a single father caught up with him. The glamour of the literary world would tug at him, and he'd find a way to escape.

"He really did cancel his tour," Izzy insisted.

Ginger saw the girl's hopeful expression, and

knew she had to banish her cynicism for Izzy's sake. The girl needed something to hope for.

Ginger looked at Marcus then, really looked at him. His face was so familiar, yet unfathomable now.

"Why don't we go inside and drum up a celebratory lunch?" she suggested. "I've been missing your avocado sandwiches."

There'd be time for questions and explanations later.

"Um, actually, I'm kind of tired," Izzy said. "I haven't slept in two nights. I was hoping I could lie down for a bit and take a nap." She glanced at Marcus as if to get his approval.

But her words had the feel of rehearsed lines, and Ginger's instincts went on alert.

"Okay," she said. "Let's get you settled then."

She picked up the carrier that held Lulu, and they went inside to Izzy's bedroom.

What she'd come to think of as Izzy's bedroom.

But now she would live somewhere else with Marcus. Ginger had allowed herself to hope that Izzy really would be hers. Whatever that meant. She'd let herself believe she would finally have the child she'd always wanted.

When she watched Izzy climb into bed and settle under the covers, her heart ached.

Marcus bent and gave Izzy a kiss on the forehead, then picked up the dog and left the room.

Ginger went to the side of the bed and sat down on the edge. She met Izzy's gaze with a gentle smile.

"Wherever you go, I want you to know you can always come back here, okay? This is your room, and this is a place you can always call home."

Izzy nodded. "Thanks," she said. "I promise I won't run away again."

"I love you." Ginger bent to give the girl a hug. "Now get some rest."

She left the room and found Marcus in the kitchen, looking tense and nervous. Lulu was on the floor devouring a bowl of dog food. When Marcus saw Ginger, he sighed.

She raised her eyebrows in a silent question.

"Can we go for a walk?" he asked.

He looked as if he hadn't slept in years, not days. And some lingering bit of tender feeling caused her to want to reach out and smooth the tension from his brow, but no. She knew better now.

"Sure," she said.

At least they had Izzy back. That was probably what he wanted to talk about. Far enough away that Izzy couldn't overhear.

He'd learned his lesson.

They went outside and walked along the path toward the lake. It was a clear, warm day with a soft breeze sweeping over the water. Sandal weather, Ruby called it.

And Ginger was wearing sandals, a pair of brown beaded flip-flops that didn't do well on the uneven gravel path. Her yellow sundress blew in the breeze, and as she walked, she tried not to be so conscious of Marcus's presence.

He was here, and she had to be okay with that for now. For Izzy's sake.

"So she was picked up for shoplifting?" Ginger asked, unable to control her curiosity any longer.

"Yeah. But I told the police her story, about losing her mom and just having met me, and they let her off with a dire warning. The owner of the 7-Eleven she tried to steal from agreed not to press charges."

"Sounds like she got lucky."

"Very. She was a wreck when I got there, crying and scared half to death."

"But…Bakersfield?" Ginger asked as they scrambled down the drop-off that led to the beach. "What was she doing there? How did she get there?"

"She hitchhiked with some trucker who was headed that way."

"Oh my God."

"By the time I got to her, she'd already had the life scared out of her by the cops about all the bad things that could have happened to her while hitchhiking."

Ginger paused once she reached the beach, and tried to get her equilibrium back. "The thought of her climbing into a truck...with some strange guy..."

"I know. I can't even think about it right now."

Marcus took Ginger's hand in his, and she resisted the urge to pull away. He led her toward the water's edge, where the sand was flat and wet. They took off their shoes and walked toward the wide stretch of beach that headed east around the lake.

"Where did she plan to go?"

Marcus told her everything he knew about Izzy's ill-thought-out scheme. The driver of the semi who took her to Bakersfield warned her not to do any more hitchhiking when he let her out at the bus station. Paralyzed with fear, she'd spent what little money she had on the cheapest ticket to L.A., but the bus didn't leave until the next day. She wandered around Bakersfield and spent the night in a park. By the following day she'd gotten hungry enough to steal, which had led to her getting busted in a convenience store for trying to shoplift a bottle of apple juice and a box of cereal.

"Wow," Ginger murmured when he finished talking.

Her anxiety over the girl's ordeal hardened into a solid knot in the pit of her stomach.

They walked in silence for a few minutes, until a piece of driftwood blocked their path. Rather than going around it, Marcus stopped walking.

"I couldn't go," he said. "I couldn't go on the book tour now. I mean, I won't go."

"Good," she said quietly. "Izzy needs you after what happened. She needs things not to change."

"You were right about me." He looked into Ginger's eyes, and she saw a depth of pain that had never been there before.

The water lapping at their feet was cool and brought with it the sensation of washing their troubles away, or their past, or both.

"What do you mean I was right?"

"I need to grow up. Needed to grow up."

"Needed?"

"I've made a few vows to myself. I'm going to be a good father to Izzy. And I'm going to make sure the people who matter to me know how I feel."

Ginger said nothing.

"That means you," he continued.

"Marcus, please…" She tried to turn away.

She didn't want to hear that he needed her because Izzy needed a mother. Much as she wanted to fill that role, she knew it wasn't a solid foundation for a relationship.

"I love you, Ginger. I've always loved you."

"That's not enough, Marcus. You know it isn't."

"I don't mean I love you as a friend. That's how I used to feel, but everything's changed. You're not the girl I used to be friends with. I've fallen in love with the woman you've become."

She wanted to brush off his words, but they rang true. Because it was exactly how she felt about him. He wasn't the man he used to be.

He wasn't running away now. He was here, trying to be a father to Izzy. He'd faced some of the most challenging circumstances a parent could imagine, and he hadn't buckled. He'd stuck with the job.

And he was telling Ginger he loved her.

He loved her.

Unlike other times in her life when she'd heard those words, now they resonated deep down in a part of her that hadn't been touched in too long.

"I love you, too," she heard herself say, before reason could jump in to stop her.

But she didn't want to stop herself. The words

felt right on her lips. She knew she meant what she'd just said.

She loved him. It was true. And it wasn't the silly, unrequited love of her college days. This was something more.

Something real.

"You do?" he said, his eyes sparking with the slightest bit of hope.

"I do."

In his eyes she could see something she'd never seen before.

Humility. It was what grief had left behind—the evidence of his trial by fire.

"I'll make it worth your while," he said.

She smiled. "I'll bet you will."

* * * * *

HARLEQUIN Super Romance

COMING NEXT MONTH

Available June 29, 2010

LARGER-PRINT BOOKS!

GET 2 FREE LARGER-PRINT NOVELS PLUS
2 FREE GIFTS!

◆HARLEQUIN®

Super Romance®

Exciting, emotional, unexpected!

HARLEQUIN®

A Romance

FOR EVERY MOOD™

Spotlight on
Heart & Home

Heartwarming romances
where love can happen
right when you least expect it.

See the next page to enjoy a sneak peek
from Silhouette Special Edition®,
a Heart and Home series.

*Introducing MCFARLANE'S PERFECT BRIDE
by USA TODAY bestselling author Christine Rimmer,
from Silhouette Special Edition®.*

Entranced. Captivated. Enchanted.

Connor sat across the table from Tori Jones and couldn't help thinking that those words exactly described what effect the small-town schoolteacher had on him. He might as well stop trying to tell himself he wasn't interested. He was powerfully drawn to her.

Clearly, he should have dated more when he was younger.

There had been a couple of other women since Jennifer had walked out on him. But he had never been entranced. Or captivated. Or enchanted.

Until now.

He wanted her—*her,* Tori Jones, in particular. Not just someone suitably attractive and well-bred, as Jennifer had been. Not just someone sophisticated, sexually exciting and discreet, which pretty much described the two women he'd dated after his marriage crashed and burned.

It came to him that he…he *liked* this woman. And that was new to him. He liked her quick wit, her wisdom and her big heart. He liked the passion in her voice when she talked about things she believed in.

He liked *her.* And suddenly it mattered all out of proportion that she might like him, too.

Was he losing it? He couldn't help but wonder. Was he cracking under the strain—of the soured economy, the McFarlane House setbacks, his divorce, the scary changes in his son? Of the changes he'd decided he needed to make in his life and himself?

Strangely, right then, on his first date with Tori Jones, he didn't care if he just might be going over the edge. He was having a great time—having *fun*, of all things—and he didn't want it to end.

Is Connor finally able to admit his feelings to Tori,
and are they reciprocated?
Find out in McFARLANE'S PERFECT BRIDE
by USA TODAY bestselling author Christine Rimmer.
Available July 2010,
only from Silhouette Special Edition®.